W9-AAD-820

"I CAN'T WORRY ABOUT YOU, KANE," Elizabeth said, her voice hoarse with emotion.

"So don't. Let me worry about me."

Her eyes glistened. "I don't think I have that choice. Not anymore." Almost to herself, she added, "I'm not sure I ever did."

Kane swore under his breath, his control so close to shattering he shook with the effort to piece the ragged edges back together. This was alien territory for him, having someone care about him. "Little Sun," he whispered, his tone rough. "Don't waste that precious energy on me. I've taken care of myself for so long, I wouldn't know what to do with it."

A sad smile lit the corners of her mouth. "That's right, the man with the empty soul." She held his gaze, her eyes burning with a fierce light deep within. "If there was ever a soul worth caring about, it is yours, Eyes of the Hawk."

He could swear he heard his control snap as he reached out and drew her to him. "Stop me."

"No." And she lifted her mouth to his. . . .

WHAT ARE *LOVESWEPT* ROMANCES?

They are stories of true romance and touching emotion. We believe those two very important ingredients are constants in our highly sensual and very believable stories in the LOVESWEPT line. Our goal is to give you, the reader, stories of consistently high quality that may sometimes make you laugh, sometimes make you cry, but are always fresh and creative and contain many delightful surprises within their pages.

Most romance fans read an enormous number of books. Those they truly love, they keep. Others may be traded with friends and soon forgotten. We hope that each LOVESWEPT romance will be a treasure—a "keeper." We will always try to publish

LOVE STORIES YOU'LL NEVER FORGET BY AUTHORS YOU'LL ALWAYS REMEMBER

The Editors

Loveswept® 707

BOUNTY HUNTER

DONNA KAUFFMAN

BANTAM BOOKS

NEW YORK · TORONTO · LONDON · SYDNEY · AUCKLAND

This book is dedicated to my editor, Beth de Guzman, and my agent,
Linda Hayes. It's been a great ride. I don't ever want to get off!

BOUNTY HUNTER
A Bantam Book / September 1994

LOVESWEPT *and the wave design are registered trademarks of*
Bantam Books, a division of Bantam Doubleday Dell Publishing Group,
Inc. Registered in U.S. Patent and Trademark Office and elsewhere.

All rights reserved.
Copyright © 1994 by Donna Kauffman.
Back cover art copyright © 1994 by Hal Frenck.
Floral border by Joyce Kitchell.
No part of this book may be reproduced or transmitted in any
form or by any means, electronic or mechanical,
including photocopying, recording, or by any
information storage and retrieval system, without
permission in writing from the publisher.
For information address: Bantam Books.

If you purchased this book without a cover you should be aware that
this book is stolen property. It was reported as "unsold and destroyed"
to the publisher and neither the author nor the publisher has received
any payment for this "stripped book."

If you would be interested in receiving protective vinyl covers for your
Loveswept books, please write to this address for information:

Loveswept
Bantam Books
P.O. Box 985
Hicksville, NY 11802

ISBN 0-553-44425-5

Published simultaneously in the United States and Canada

Bantam Books are published by Bantam Books, a division of Bantam Dou-
bleday Dell Publishing Group, Inc. Its trademark, consisting of the words
"Bantam Books" and the portrayal of a rooster, is Registered in U.S.
Patent and Trademark Office and in other countries. Marca Registrada.
Bantam Books, 1540 Broadway, New York, New York 10036.

PRINTED IN THE UNITED STATES OF AMERICA
OPM   0 9 8 7 6 5 4 3 2 1

PROLOGUE

"Find my wife, and I'll make sure you never want for anything in your life."

Kane Hawthorne studied the bank president seated behind the large mahogany desk: Tailored pin-striped suit, tailored haircut, tailored smile. Everything about Sam Perkins was calculated to elicit trust. Calculated being the operative word. In Kane's world, trust was a rare commodity that had to be earned.

"My fee plus expenses will be enough. Half now, the rest in a secured account in another bank, paid on delivery." Kane's attention remained fixed on the smaller man. Something wasn't right. Kane's focused intensity had been known to unnerve most men. He'd used it to his advantage often and never took it for granted. But Perkins's gaze didn't waver, nor did he seem to mind being scrutinized. His expression was faintly smug, superior.

"I'm going to need more information," Kane said quietly.

"Whatever it takes. I just want her found and brought back to me before something happens to her."

Kane went on full alert. "You said she ran because you cut off her line of credit. You think she's in danger?"

Perkins smiled. "Elizabeth may be beautiful, but . . . well, you know how women are with money. She thought that because I run the bank, I'm loaded. I simply wanted to make a point, but Elizabeth is impulsive. She can be very temperamental when she doesn't get her way. I'm afraid she'll do something foolish to spite me. I want her back safe and sound before she gets mixed up in something she can't handle."

"Sounds as if you'd be better off without her," Kane observed, his voice flat, devoid of emotion.

An odd light flickered briefly in Perkins's eyes, and it struck Kane that it was the first honest emotion he'd detected in the man.

Passion. It existed in Sam Perkins. But what inspired it? His young wife? Was that why Perkins was so hot to have her back? A bed could get real cold at night in Idaho. Kane felt a distinct chill.

"All the facts, Perkins. Or I walk."

"Fine. I need her back. Without her, I'm nothing."

Kane glanced at the blond woman smiling gaily up at him from a gold-plated frame on the desk. His gaze moved to Perkins's hands. White knuckles showed against the strain of gripping the edge of that same desk.

No, this was a man with a score to settle. He wanted his lovely, money-grubbing wife back so badly, he'd give up anything to get her. Why? What difference did it make?

It was just another job.

He looked Perkins in the eye. "You've got yourself a bounty hunter."

ONE

"Preserved by Ann." Elizabeth Lawson sat back on her heels and mopped the sweat from her neck. "No," she muttered to herself, "sounds like a weird embalmer." She shoved the damp bandanna in the rear pocket of her jeans and reached for another bristly vine. "Ann's Jams. Nah. Even dumber." She plucked three plump raspberries. One went into her mouth, and the other two into the basket sitting in front of her knees.

"Eating the profits isn't good business."

Elizabeth shrieked and lurched forward, dumping over four hours of back-aching work onto the dusty ground. The strange deep voice had come out of nowhere, making her forget her usual wariness. "Look what you made me do!" she cried, scrambling to her feet. "Do you have any idea how long it took me to fill—"

Her tirade died on the light summer wind as she

looked up at her unexpected visitor. She had to look higher than the late-afternoon sun before her gaze connected with his.

"I apologize," he said, his tone more flat than sincere.

Elizabeth was staring at him, too overcome by his sheer presence to speak. Long hair black as midnight, eyes even darker. His face and forearms were the even color of a man who was likely bronzed all over. He wore a red bandanna tied at the throat, an open-collared blue chambray shirt, battered jeans, and dusty boots that had seen better days. She skimmed back over his rough-hewn frame to his face, unable to tamp down the idea that this man looked more savage in beat-up ranch clothes than any other man would in a breechcloth.

His gaze was fixed on her, its concentrated energy a bit rattling. She couldn't tell if her close perusal bothered him, or if he'd even noticed.

"I'll replace the loss."

His deep, even-timbred voice snapped Elizabeth from her thoughts. Heat from an inner source colored cheeks already reddened by the sun. Where had he come from? Why hadn't she heard him approach? She hadn't even heard his truck.

She didn't respond to his offer. "Who are you?" she demanded, her tone wary. "What do you want?"

"Kane Hawthorne," he responded immediately, though his expression remained unchanged. "And if you're Ann Fielding, then what I want is to help you."

Ann Fielding. She still wasn't used to that name. Suspicion flooded Elizabeth's mind. She fought the sudden tightening of her chest and willed her hands to stay relaxed at her side. Trapped. It was a feeling she'd become intimate with over the last three months. She didn't like it now any more than when she'd fled Boise in fear of her life.

"Help with what?" She hoped he didn't notice the slight tremor in her voice.

"Dobson down at the general store said you might be needing help with your barn. Said you were thinking of renovating it so you could expand."

Elizabeth wanted to believe him. Being suspicious of everyone and everything went against her nature, and she was plain sick and tired of it. But trust was a luxury. A life-and-death matter even. Hers. And as much as she would have liked some help, she couldn't afford it—or take the risk of hiring an outsider.

"I'm sorry if Dobs misled you," she began, "but I'm not hiring right now."

"You are Ann Fielding?"

She shaded her eyes and looked straight at him. "Yes. But I'm not hiring. Sorry."

He didn't say anything, simply bent down and began picking up the berries that hadn't rolled in the dirt.

Surprised as much by his actions as by the image

of those delicate red berries being plucked by thick, work-roughened fingers, Elizabeth didn't speak right away. After a moment spent watching him, she almost crouched beside him to help, but quickly decided against it. She might never have a height advantage over him again, so she figured she'd make the most of this opportunity.

"You might try the Double Y," she suggested, struggling to sound casual. "I heard Dobs say that the Yancy brothers are looking for someone to help wrangle."

"He told me," he said, still gathering stray berries.

She stared at the dark hair that fell well past his collar as he continued picking up raspberries. Her patience began to fray. "What, you don't like cows?"

"I've got nothing against cows."

She waited a beat, then said, "Well?"

He stood. The motion was fluid with a grace she wouldn't have attributed to someone his size. He faced her. "Figured you needed me more than they did."

Before she could respond, he turned and headed toward the ramshackle barn about a hundred yards away.

She watched his easy gait for all of ten seconds before she realized exactly which part of his "gait" had captured her attention. "Hey, wait a minute," she called, then hurried after him when he showed no signs of slowing. "Stop!"

He did. But not until he'd reached the barn doors. Or what was left of them. They were both rusted and warped with a space between them barely wide enough for her to squeeze through. He grabbed one side.

"Don't bother pulling. I've worked on that for weeks. It needs to be dismantled, I guess."

Kane spared her a glance, then bent to the task at hand. One mighty yank and the door squealed back far enough to allow both of them to enter side by side if they chose.

Elizabeth spent a second longer marveling at the abundant strength he carried along with that quiet demeanor. It must be nice to have that sort of power to call upon whenever the need arose, she thought, a bit annoyed. She knew if she let him see her irritation, he would somehow turn it around as a testimony to her need for help. She swallowed another portion of pride and pasted on a smile. "Thanks."

His lips remained a flat line, but she could have sworn there was a hint of a twinkle in his dark eyes as he nodded and motioned her ahead of him with a low swept arm.

She wandered inside before it occurred to her to ask why he wanted to see inside her barn in the first place.

It was musty and dank. The weathered boards had warped allowing long slivers of light to cut across the hay-strewn dirt floor. She'd only taken a few steps, but it was enough to stir up dust motes, and she paused to wave her hand in front of her face to clear the air.

When she looked up again, she saw that Kane was circling the ancient tractor rusting quietly in the open area between the run-down stalls.

"It's as bad as it looks," she commented, as she crossed the room to stand on the other side of the tractor.

He looked up, his gaze meeting hers across the cracked leather seat. "You never know. Looks can be deceiving."

Elizabeth shrugged, trying not to examine his statement for hidden meanings. "I think my biggest concern with this old heap will be how to move it out of the way."

He didn't respond, but turned his attention back to the tractor.

Elizabeth blew out a silent breath. Trying to figure out what was going on behind that stoic gaze of his was beginning to irritate her. She wandered over to the few remaining stalls at the opposite end of the barn.

She had to get rid of this guy.

"These look salvageable."

Again she started, banging her elbow against the stall door hanging drunkenly on one hinge. "How do you do that?"

"Do what?"

He was barely a foot away. Her pulse picked up speed. She shivered and rubbed her sore elbow, fighting the impulse to cross her arms over her chest. It had to be near ninety degrees inside the barn. The goose bumps stayed. "You sneak up on people without making any sound."

"I wasn't sneaking. You were merely distracted. How long have you been living out here?"

The change in topic threw her. But she rallied quickly. It was a simple question, really. Understandable, even. But suddenly Elizabeth didn't want to answer any more of his questions. "I don't see where that is any of your business, Mr. . . . I'm sorry, what did you say your name was?"

"Hawthorne. Kane Hawthorne. I guess I'm not doing too great with this job interview, am I?"

Elizabeth felt her mouth drop open. He'd actually smiled. And he looked almost . . . handsome, if someone with such focused energy could be called something so bland. It suddenly occurred to her that she probably shouldn't be alone in the barn with a strange man. Of course, being outside wouldn't be much better, she reminded herself. Four miles of hard mountain road stood between her and Dobson's little store and the Boundary Gap post office.

And yet, she realized she wasn't afraid of him. At least, not in the physical sense. She glanced quickly at his broad frame, remembering the bunched muscles of his biceps as he'd yanked open the barn door. Her gaze fell to his big, strong hands. In a way it really was a shame she couldn't hire him on. "I'm truly sorry, but as I explained earlier—"

He stepped forward. A sliver of light slashed

across his bronzed features. Elizabeth drew in a ragged breath and instinctively stepped backward. Her hip bumped against the hanging door.

"It's obvious you need help, if you want to get your canning operation off the ground." At her raised eyebrow, he added, "Dobs told me about your famous preserves." He went on without letting her speak. "If you can't afford to pay me, we can always work out a barter system."

Goose bumps lined her skin again as images came to her mind of what she had to barter with. Maybe she'd been wrong about being in physical danger. She lifted her chin and leveled him with her best glare. "I think you'd better leave now."

He actually had the grace to look . . . well, she wouldn't call it embarrassed exactly, but he did shift his dark eyes away from her.

Lord, but the man was intense. And intensity usually equaled stress. More stress, she did not need. She moved to slip by him, intending to head outside, hoping he'd take the hint and leave without making a scene.

"What are those things on your knees?"

She froze, then slowly looked downward. "Sponges." She stifled a groan.

"That's what I thought."

She squeezed her eyes shut as a mental vision of what she must look like flashed in her mind. Her pinned-up shoulder-length hair once had been #74R Auburn Dream, but now, after an overly enthusiastic home perm, looked more like Ronald Mc-

Donald Red. To make matters worse, she had on a raggedy, juice-stained T-shirt, abused designer jeans that even acid washing wouldn't help, and big orange car-washing sponges strapped to her knees.

She smiled ruefully and opened her eyes to look at him. "I think I owe you an apology."

"What for? You use them for knee pads, right?"

"Yes. But I meant for my earlier assumption that you were angling to trade work for . . ." Her voice trailed off as the lightest of twinkles flickered in his black eyes. If she'd been embarrassed moments ago, it was nothing compared to the humiliation she felt now.

It must have shown on her face, because his lips curved a bit more and he leaned over and rubbed at a spot on her cheek.

"I imagine you clean up just fine." As suddenly as it had appeared, his smile fled. He dropped his hand and stepped away. "But you're right, that wasn't what I meant. No offense."

"No," she said, her voice cracking. She was a bit short of breath for some reason. She cleared her throat and tried again. "None taken."

"I also think you should reconsider." He held up his hand to stop her automatic denial. "I'm looking for a place to stay just for a while. A few weeks, a month at the most. I noticed you have a small bunkhouse behind the barn."

"It's hardly habitable," she replied. But any hope she had of gaining control of the conversation was short-lived.

"If you take me on, I'll take care of that on my own time. I can restore enough of the barn so that you can move your working operation out here. I'll be glad to do other small repairs on the ranch house, if you need them done." His tone implied it would be pointless to argue. "In return, you let me stay in the bunkhouse, maybe throw in an occasional meal."

Take him on? A man like Kane Hawthorne? Elizabeth could come up with a dozen reasons why she shouldn't—two dozen. And not all of them had to do with her current predicament. But it was hard to ignore the single reason why she should. The fact was, he was offering her the best solution to her problems she could ever hope to have.

The money she'd taken from her brother's apartment was almost gone, and she didn't know when he'd be back in the country. Selling in bulk the preserves she made with her grandmother's family recipe was her best shot at supporting herself until Matthew came back from his latest overseas assignment.

If she was willing to take the risk of hiring Kane.

She studied him. Judging from his clothes and his physique, he was no stranger to hard labor. But the fact remained that he was a total stranger. Elizabeth gritted her teeth in frustration. More than anything in the world, she wanted to not have to question people's motives, not to see potential danger lurking in every corner. It was an exhausting lifestyle, and she resented the hell out of being forced into adopting it.

Of course, if Kane proved to be trustworthy, it might not be a bad idea to have someone like him around for a while, in case Sam or one of his hired goons managed to track her down. And if Matt surfaced during that time, then all her problems would be solved anyway.

She wavered, glancing away as she mentally calculated increased profits versus how much a man his size might eat.

"If you want references, I can provide a few names for you to contact."

She jerked her gaze to his. "Why are you here?" she asked, then added, "I don't mean here on the Lazy F, I mean in this area. It's pretty barren this far north, and with fall coming, these mountains aren't going to get any friendlier."

"Guess I'm what you'd call a wanderer. Can't seem to find any one place that interests me enough to make me want to stay. I move when I want, work when I can, then move on again. I like it that way.

"Sounds lonely to me."

"If I want to be around people, I go where there's people."

"I didn't say alone. I said lonely. Big difference."

"Sounds to me like it might be more your problem than mine."

His uncanny perception rattled her, but Elizabeth shoved that fact aside and focused on the decision at hand. "So you want to help me because restoring a barn is more interesting than wrangling cows?"

"Didn't say that. But if you're asking me if you're more interesting to me than a herd of cattle, then I'd have to say yes. Yes, you are."

Elizabeth gripped the beam next to her shoulder, wondering how big a mistake she was about to make. Possibly bigger than the one she'd made the night she'd decided to follow Sam to one of his frequent late-night meetings. A mistake that had forced her to run for her life.

"The only materials you'll have to work with are whatever you can scrounge up from the outbuildings. I don't have money to invest in building supplies. I can't promise to fill your stomach every night, but if I have enough for two, you're welcome to share." She turned away and headed toward the barn door, forcing herself to breathe evenly and walk slowly. *What was she doing?* "Oh, and I do want that list of references."

She'd walked several yards away from the barn when he spoke from behind her. "I'll get them to you before nightfall. But if you don't mind, I'd like to check out the buildings and make a list of the materials—"

She whirled around. "I thought I'd made it clear—"

"You did," he broke in quietly. "But my bartering skills aren't limited to getting a stubborn redhead to admit she needs help in exchange for room and board."

It was on the tip of her tongue to correct him about her hair color. Being a redhead was a new experience. An old adage proved correct. If the life she'd led since the day she'd left Boise was any indication, blondes most definitely had more fun.

She put her hands on her hips, determined to take charge before things got any further out of hand. "Fine. Just don't trade away anything on this property without asking me first. And you might think about finding a place to sleep before it gets dark. I have running water piped in from an uphill stream, but my propane is limited, so no hot water unless it's necessary. No electricity, either. I have to pick another couple of quarts of berries, so I can't promise you dinner tonight. If you need a place to store any of your gear until you get the bunkhouse livable, let me know. I'll make room for it in the house." She paused for a breath.

"Yes, ma'am."

She squinted in the sun, but was unable to determine from either his expression or his tone if he was teasing her. Somehow, she didn't think he was the type. And to her eternal dismay she found herself wondering just what type he was.

Kane watched Ann Fielding walk away from him. His instincts and his research left very little doubt that she was actually Elizabeth Lawson-Perkins.

So why wasn't he heading back to Boise with her

in tow? A whole lot of money was waiting there for him. All he had to do was hand her over to Sam Perkins, take his fee, and walk away. Walk away. Yeah, he was a real pro at that.

Kane shook his head and turned on his heel, taking off around the old ranch house and heading for the big bay mare he'd left tied to the porch railing. He'd been so distracted by his mixed reaction to Ms. Lawson-Perkins that he'd neglected to mention the horse.

Rubbing her muzzle, Kane spoke to her softly in his native tongue, glad she'd been available when he'd needed to ditch his truck in a hurry. He unstrapped his duffel bag and saddle packs, then loosened the cinch on the saddle. He hung it over the sturdiest section of porch railing, scooped up his gear, and headed around the house. Telling her about the horse was going to be the least of his problems.

Kane didn't even bother ignoring the jolt his system received from observing her lush backside as she bent on her hands and knees to pick more berries. It was a position that brought an immediate answer to his earlier mental query.

He wasn't dragging her to Boise because his brains had gone south for the summer. He'd be lying if he said his reaction to her hadn't surprised the hell out of him. He'd hardly expected a wild-haired redhead with brand-new freckles, scrabbling around in the bushes for wild berries, sporting sponges for knee pads. He'd also been surprised to learn that on the right woman, freckles could be sexy as sin.

Of course, she wasn't the right woman.

Not for him, at any rate. She was a wanted woman. A married, wanted woman.

But one look had been enough to confirm his suspicions of three weeks earlier as he'd stood in Perkins's office. This was no errant wife with a grudge. And until he figured out what the hell was really going on, he was a hired hand on the Lazy F.

Elizabeth cast a wary glance at the barn. After Kane had all but splintered the remains of the bunkhouse door several hours before, he'd dumped his gear inside and headed into the rickety building. She heard several thumps and a few loud crashes, but avoided giving in to the temptation to go inside and find out what he was doing. Being alone with him in that dark, steamy barn again was not a good idea.

She stood and arched her back, massaging her spine with her gloved fingers. She checked the sun and figured she had just enough time to rinse off the day's harvest in the clear spring that spouted from a tumble of rocks up the hill behind the barn. Groaning as she stooped to grab the bucket, she froze in midpull as a high whinnying sound echoed across the yard.

She could have sworn it sounded like a horse. Not all that uncommon in this area of northern

Idaho, but considering the nearest ranch was over the next ridge, it *was* a bit surprising. The horse whinnied again, and without thinking, Elizabeth set the bucket down and headed toward the front of the small, four-room ranch house.

Beside the rusty old pickup truck she'd gone to unbelievable lengths to purchase, was a huge bay mare with white spots splashed across her rump. She walked over to her, pulled off one glove, and held up her hand. The horse nuzzled her bare palm. "Sorry, girl, I don't have anything for you."

Someone, and she had to assume it was Kane, since there was no other car around, had tied the horse to her porch and slung the saddle over the remaining section of railing that hadn't dry-rotted or fallen apart from neglect.

She stroked the lush black mane. "No wonder I didn't hear him coming."

A dark forearm snaked past her shoulder, a hand much larger than hers ran down the mare's neck.

"I should have mentioned her earlier."

Elizabeth jumped, then stilled, barely swallowing the shriek that had risen in her throat. She told herself it was his bad habit of sneaking up on her, not his deep baritone voice, that did unnatural things to her blood pressure. "Yes, you should have," she managed at length.

"She won't be any trouble, I take full responsibility for her maintenance."

"Fine." She didn't doubt he'd be true to his

word. The horse probably wouldn't be any trouble. But considering the way her heart pounded every time Kane got within three feet of her, she had to wonder if the same could be said of the mare's owner.

TWO

"I cleared out a place in the barn for her. Hope you don't mind."

Unsettled by his nearness, Elizabeth simply nodded.

Kane didn't say anything else. He slipped the lead from the railing and hefted the saddle to his shoulder. He'd led the mare halfway to the side of the house before she found her voice.

"I'm making vegetable stew tonight."

He paused, but didn't look back right away. She took the moment to admire how straight his back was, how wide his shoulders, how nicely his jeans—*Whoa*. Maybe Kane had hit a little too close to home with his comment about her loneliness. She'd admit that her prolonged isolation was a part of why she'd accepted his offer, even when she knew the risks outweighed the benefits. But that didn't mean she was foolish enough to let herself think about Kane in any way other than as a capable pair of hands helping her in a time of need.

He turned slightly, and even from a distance she felt the impact of his gaze. "I'd like to get a few more things done before it gets too dark. If that suits your plans, then I'd appreciate the meal."

Again all she could do was nod. He nodded in return, and she stared after him until he disappeared around the side of the house. She started to climb the stairs to the sagging porch but remembered she'd forgotten her bucket.

She scanned the field beyond the barn as she crossed the backyard, but found no sign of Kane or his horse. She shrugged off the vague sense of disappointment and retrieved the berries. It was getting a bit late, and she decided to forgo rinsing them in the spring. She'd use some of the water from the tank in the house.

She picked up speed as she crossed the yard and went through the back door into the small antiquated kitchen. She pulled down a colander from a hook on the wall, gently dumped the berries inside, and pumped enough water to half fill the bucket. After carefully rinsing them, she wiped her hands on a towel and set about quickly chopping vegetables and tossing them into the iron kettle on the propane stove. It wasn't until she'd dumped in some herbs and turned to lift a handful of berries that she realized she was rushing so she'd have time to make dessert before Kane arrived.

She rationalized that she'd more than earned the

treat as she gathered the ingredients for cobbler. She certainly wasn't trying to impress her newly hired hand. But she'd also be lying if she said she wasn't looking forward to sharing a meal. The novelty of cooking for one—of cooking at all—had worn off after her first week here.

Her smile faltered as thoughts of Sam entered her mind. He'd hated finding her in the kitchen the few times she'd ventured into that gleaming chrome room in his posh home. He said the job of a bank president's wife was to be the hostess, not the chef, even if they were the only two dining.

Elizabeth shivered for the third time that afternoon, only this time the reason was pure dread. It seemed so clear to her now. It made her stomach churn when she thought of how flattered she'd felt by Sam's constant attention. After her initial panic had receded and she'd fled Matthew's apartment for the Lazy F, she'd spent long hours trying to convince herself that any woman would have responded to Sam's lavish care that way, would have taken his small, but constant suggestions about everything from her clothing to cosmetics as a sign of his devotion, as she had. Instead of as the early warning signals they really were; signs that something wasn't quite right.

The back screen door slapped against the wood frame, and Kane Hawthorne stepped into the tiny kitchen.

"Sorry if I startled you. I knocked but I guess you didn't hear."

Elizabeth wasn't sure why this man, a dark stranger with the most compelling eyes she'd ever seen, made her suddenly feel safer than she'd felt in a long time. She didn't bother to analyze it, not wanting to ruin her first shared meal in months. "You seem to have a talent for catching me with my head in the clouds. If you need to wash up—"

"Done. I found a spring up the slope behind the barn. I let the mare loose on the far side of the barn. There were no bramble thickets around, so your crop should be safe."

"Thanks, that was very considerate of you. Everything's just about ready, if you want to have a seat." She gestured to the small wooden table. It canted a bit on one side, but it was scrubbed clean and otherwise was serviceable enough.

"Smells good in here." His large frame dwarfed the wooden chair.

She turned back to the stove, unable to keep the small triumphant smile from creeping across her face. "After being in that musty barn, I imagine anything would smell better."

She turned in time to catch him staring at her again. She averted her gaze and set two small salads and a basket of bread on the table next to the crock of butter. She watched him stare at his salad for a moment, then at the bread, then finally up at her again.

"I know it might seem redundant to have a salad

before vegetable stew, but . . ." She shrugged uncertainly as he continued to stare at her. It should
have made her feel uncomfortable, and in a tingling,
warm sort of way, she guessed it did.

She finally turned her attention to the rolls.
"Help yourself. I wish I could say I made them, but
I traded some jam for them at Dobs's store."

Kane's hand reached out and engulfed the small
glass jar sitting next to the butter crock. He lifted it
and inspected it. "So, this is the legendary jam everyone's raving about?"

She felt the warmth in her cheeks as he looked at
her. "I don't know about raving. But people seem to
like it enough to buy it."

"It must be something, if you need room to
make more. Boundary Gap isn't exactly overrun
with tourists, or residents in need of jam, for that
matter."

"It was sort of a fluke. I, uh, noticed that the
thickets bordering the fields were a goldmine of
berries. So far I've found wild raspberries, huckle-
berries, lingonberries, even some wild plums—"
She stopped short when she realized she was bab-
bling. *The man asks a simple question, and I sound like
Peterson's Guide to Edible Fruit.* "Anyway," she said,
forcing a more casual note, "I scrounged around in
here and found Grandma Fielding's recipes for preserves. I took some to Dobs to . . . well, to trade."
She faltered for a moment, suddenly uncomfortable
with just how much her story was revealing about
her predicament.

"Sounds as if I'm not the only one with bartering skills around here."

He didn't smile, but his comment sounded sincere and went a long way toward easing the sudden tension.

"Well, to make a long story short, Dobs sold some to a woman who was traveling in the area looking for local crafts to sell at some of the fairs farther south, around Sandpoint and Coeur d'Alene. She liked it and thought it would be a good seller. Dobs knew I needed . . . well, he was nice enough to pass the word on to me. Then there's Kootenai River Days later this month, and Bonners Ferry has a Boundary County Fair. So now I have less than a month to come up with as many jars of jam and preserves as I can."

She realized he had been listening politely to her excited rush of words instead of eating. Her cheeks colored slightly, and she gestured to the basket of rolls. "Why don't you try some and let me know what you think?"

"You going to join me?"

Elizabeth ignored the ridiculous spurt of pleasure his innocent request caused and lifted the stew to the table. Sitting down across from him, she said, "Yes, of course."

She noticed he waited for her to take a roll and butter it before he did the same. He began eating as soon as she'd taken the first bite. She swallowed and said, "Your mother raised a gentleman, I see." The words had sort of tumbled out. She wasn't prepared for the storm clouds that crossed his face as the fork he was holding paused in midair. After a moment he continued the motion.

He was silent as he ate, the frown less visible now. He laid his fork down and picked up a roll, buttering it lightly before spreading on the jam. Elizabeth couldn't seem to stop staring at him. She realized she wasn't even making a pretense of eating. What had she said to make him tense up? Did she dare come out and ask?

He made short work of the roll. "This is really good," he said quietly as if nothing had happened. "I understand the demand."

"Thank you." She finally looked away and tried to eat. Maybe she'd imagined his reaction earlier.

"My grandmother was famous for her dried sweet fruit. It was known on the reservation that receiving a gift of a fruit basket from Cloud Dancer meant good luck would follow," he said.

"Cloud Dancer. Pretty name. Which reservation? Wind River? Duck Valley?"

"Fort Hall. I am half Shoshone on my mother's side. My father was British Columbian."

"Was? He's gone?" she asked, then quickly said, "I'm sorry, that was rude. It's just, well, my folks died when I was a teenager and so I know how it feels . . ."

After a long pause, he said, "He's not dead. Not as far as I know, anyway. He left my mother before I was born to go work pipeline in Alaska. I'm pretty sure she never expected him to return."

"So, you grew up at Fort Hall?"

Now he concentrated on his stew. "For the most part. I left when I was seventeen." *And never went back.*

He hadn't spoken the last part out loud, but Elizabeth could hear the words so clearly, he might as well have. "It must have been hard for you on your own."

"I managed well enough."

"Still, I don't know what I'd have done without Matthew after my folks died."

"Matthew?"

"My older brother." She smiled as she spoke of him. "He stuck with me, worked so I could go to school. Now he works for the government. Hush-hush stuff, he calls it."

"Sounds like you both did okay. Do you see him much?"

"Not as often as I'd like. But he devoted so much of his life to me, I can hardly complain."

"Nothing wrong with admitting you miss some-one you love."

She looked up, but his dark eyes were trained on his food. She wondered what he was seeing, doubt-ing it was her stew. Did he miss someone he loved? "No," she said softly, tamping down her sudden in-terest in him. "I suppose not."

Her throat burned for a moment as reality came crashing back in around her. Kane's sudden arrival in her life pointed out to her just how far she had yet to go in accepting her forced isolation. She was undeniably intrigued by him, found herself wanting to ask him questions about his past, his heritage. But was it Kane, the man, she was interested in, or did she simply want someone to talk to?

It was a moot point since she wouldn't have the luxury of finding out. His steady voice jerked her from her thoughts.

"I checked the barn as thoroughly as I could. I think with some simple repairs, the front half can be salvaged fairly easily. But the rest is a loss without major work."

She appreciated his bluntness almost as much as the change of topic. "I won't need much room. Fix what you can and I'm sure it'll be fine." For some reason she decided not to tell him that she wasn't planning on staying long enough to make a complete overhaul of the barn worthwhile.

She started as his chair scraped across the uneven flooring. Kane stood and carried his plates to the counter. She watched as he primed the small pump by the sink, momentarily too caught up in the play of muscles in his arm and shoulder to tell him to stop.

He turned back to her before she could look away. "If you're done, I'll be glad to wash these."

She sensed it would be important to a man like Kane to pull his own weight, but the kitchen felt suddenly stifling, more intimate than cramped, and she couldn't see herself standing close to him, drying dishes as he washed. She quickly stood. "Thanks, but really, it's not necessary. I would've been washing these anyway. A few more won't take much longer."

He seemed about to say something, then apparently thought better of it, because he handed her the dishtowel. "Thank you for the meal. Will you be picking berries again tomorrow?"

"Only in the morning. I plan to cook all afternoon."

"Won't it get hot in here?"

"I'd rather be in here cooking than outside in the heat of the day."

"You were out there today."

"I know, but I needed to get enough berries to get a head start tomorrow."

"And I made you dump half of them."

She waved away his concern. "Don't worry, there's plenty more where those came from." He started to say something else, but she cut him off. "Really. With what I get in the morning, I'll have more than enough to start. I really can't handle more until I have more room."

"I'll let you know as soon as I make some headway."

"Fine."

He paused, and for a long moment, Elizabeth didn't know what to do or say.

"If you don't mind, I'll take a look in here when you're out in the fields tomorrow, see what I can repair."

Kane. Alone in her house? "I'd really rather have you work on the—"

"I'll get the barn done. But this house looks as if it hasn't been lived in for decades—"

"It's been twenty-five years."

"Well, if this room is anything to go by, I'm sure you wouldn't mind having a few things repaired. Consider it thanks for feeding me."

"But you're already earning—"

"My room by fixing your barn," he finished. "I'll earn the rest in here."

Elizabeth couldn't stop the shiver from racing lightly over her skin as images she had no right visualizing persisted in crowding into her brain. The sensation ceased, but the mental pictures left her skin damp. She wanted to pluck at her shirt, but didn't dare draw his attention to her sudden discomfort.

"Fine," was all she could manage.

He tilted his head in a brief nod. The next moment, she was standing alone.

Perversely, now that she'd gotten what she wanted, she wished she'd kept him talking longer. She turned to the dishes with a sigh.

And later that night, when she slid into her grandmother's lumpy feather bed, she worked hard to shut out images of Kane wandering through her house.

If dreams were any indication, she was less than successful.

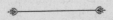

The muscles in Kane's shoulders burned as he bent his weight against the stubborn plank. With a loud grunt and a mighty yank, Kane snapped the board off. The resounding crack echoed throughout the barn.

"Figures the only boards I have to pull are the ones the termites left behind," he grumbled as he tossed the scrap in the growing heap behind him.

He'd found a pile of rusty tools in the small shed beside the barn. They were very outdated, but functional. And thanks to Cloud Dancer and her insistence that, as a child, Kane learn to function with tools made of his own hand, these would be more than adequate.

"If she could only see me now," he muttered. Thinking of the recalcitrant adolescent he'd been after his mother died, he allowed himself a small sad smile as he yanked the next board from its moorings.

His thoughts strayed to his "employer," Ann Fielding. He grunted more than necessary, and another plank went flying. He should be getting used to it. He'd hardly thought of anything else since he'd left her in that poor excuse for a kitchen the night before. And he'd be less than honest if he said his thoughts had been of a strictly professional nature.

She'd revealed more to him by simply existing out here on this rugged scrap of wilderness she called a ranch, than by coming right out with the information about her family and current financial circumstances. Somewhere between the salad and the stew, he'd forgotten he was subtly interrogating her and had actually been listening because he was truly interested.

He almost growled as he ripped the next board from the posts in front of him. Because of that gross error in judgment, he'd spent the night wrestling with his sleeping bag and his conscience. But now it was a new day, and his head was as clear as the sky. He was here to do a job. Simple.

His gaze strayed to the door that led to her kitchen and the bucket he'd left sitting on her stoop. He glanced at the horizon. It was well after seven and there was no sign of her yet.

What in the hell was she doing out in the middle of nowhere? His instincts as well as his eyes told him that Sam Perkins knew next to nothing about his wife if he thought she would crumple without a gold card.

But then again, maybe Sam Perkins knew more about his wife than he'd let on. It wouldn't surprise Kane. Especially in light of the fact that Sam hadn't bothered to mention he was having him tailed. Kane had managed to lose the hired goon just north of Coeur d'Alene. At that point, he hadn't known exactly where the Lazy F was located, but until he'd figured out Sam's angle, he sure as hell wasn't going to lead the guy straight to it. So he'd traded his pickup for a horse. A horse didn't have tags and a registration that could be traced.

Hinges squeaked across the yard behind him.

Kane stilled, willing himself not to look. He knew she was discovering his offering and suddenly wished he were somewhere else.

"Kane?"

Her soft voice floating on the clear morning air rode his senses like sweet music. "Damn," he swore under his breath as his body responded to the sound of her crossing the stretch of land separating them. This was insane. He should just haul her back and dump her on Perkins, grab his money, and head out in search of another client who required his special skills.

"Kane?" she called again from a few feet away.

He didn't feel too damn special right now. Steeling himself, he looked up at her. And he knew then that he wasn't taking her anywhere. Not yet.

On the heels of that decision came the knowledge that the only place he *did* want to take her was to bed.

His gaze skimmed over her plain white T-shirt, stopping briefly at the conspicuous designer label on her wrinkled pleated shorts. A testimony to her recent change in circumstances. On someone else, the ensemble would have looked rumpled and mismatched. On her it was sexy. As if she'd just rolled out of bed and pulled on clothes tossed carelessly away in the heat of passion.

Passion. Heat. Damn if she didn't stir both in him.

The final irony was that she was the first to do so

in a very long time. Maybe ever. And she was legally bound to another man.

He pulled his gaze away from her, hating the effort involved. "Yes?" he answered finally.

"You didn't need to do this."

Knowing she meant the bucket of raspberries he'd gotten up at dawn to pick, he kept his eyes trained on sorting the pieces of wood into usable lumber and scrap. "Yes. I did."

She didn't respond right away. "Well, then, thank you."

"No problem." He was done sorting and knew he couldn't go on with his work without looking at her. He mentally cursed himself for his cowardice. Cloud Dancer would have been vastly amused to see her stoic grandson behaving like an untried brave, hiding his face for fear some soft emotion shone in his eyes. That thought alone brought his head up and his gaze to hers.

Business. This was just business as usual.

"Do you still need to go in the fields?" he asked, his voice more terse than he'd intended.

"For an hour or so." She smiled and lifted the bucket a bit. "This will cut at least an hour of work off my day though."

He nodded and said, "If it's okay with you then, I'll go inside and check out the rooms."

If he hadn't been studying her so closely, he would have missed the slight blush that briefly colored her cheeks. Was she so used to her wealthy lifestyle that she was embarrassed for him to see her humble surroundings? She hadn't made any excuses the previous night at dinner.

"Is there any part of the house that needs to be worked on first?" She fidgeted with the bucket handle, and another thought occurred to him. "Or a part you'd rather me not go into?"

She blushed again. And damn if he didn't respond. So, she was uncomfortable with the idea of him invading her privacy. He wondered what in the hell she'd do if he told her just how privately he'd thought about invading her space. His thoughts must have flashed in his eyes, because she stepped back.

"Ah, no, you can go anywhere you want." She laughed a bit dryly. "And as to what needs to be fixed, take your pick."

"This place looks as if it's survived for quite a while."

She smiled softly. "I guess it has. Grandpa Fielding died just after he and Grandma had homesteaded this property. That was over fifty years ago. Grandma tried for years, even after my mom married and moved away, to make it into a working proposition, but it never panned out. I'd been here only once before. I was about seven. My folks dragged me and my brother up here to try to convince Grandma to come and live with us. It took us a few weeks, but she gave in. No one's been back up here since."

"Why didn't they sell it?"

"I don't know. Maybe my folks never got around

to it, or maybe no one wanted it. After they died, neither Matt nor I really gave it any thought."

Until she needed a place to run to. Kane thought about the picture in his saddlebag. He knew what she'd looked like around age seven. He knew because he'd searched her brother's apartment and found an old black-and-white photo of them standing together under the Lazy F sign that still hung over the entrance to the long, winding driveway. Elizabeth Ann Lawson, the child, had been all blond pigtails, freckles, and scuffed knees. He hadn't known she'd never been back since, but it had been his only lead.

And Elizabeth Ann Lawson-Perkins, the grown woman, had just handed him a golden opportunity to get a confession as to why she'd run in the first place. Run from a man who was paying him to bring her back.

"What made you come back here after all that time?" He watched the lovely pink hue on her cheeks fade to white. He swallowed the urge to apologize for upsetting her.

Instead he silently watched her struggle for control.

She tilted her chin and pasted a spectacular and patently false smile across her face. "I guess I got tired of the rat race and decided to get back to nature for a while. You know, get in touch with my feelings and all that." She glanced around her. "Of course, I didn't want to touch nature quite so closely, but this was the only place I knew to go."

She'd been all bravado until that last part of her admission, which had come out on more of a waver.

Kane felt a tug in the middle of his chest which he steadfastly ignored. Just as he ignored the sudden urge to pull her into his arms and tell her it would be all right, that he'd protect her.

What in the hell had gotten into him? He clenched his fists at his sides to keep from reaching for her, his blunt nails digging into his palms. "Did someone hurt you? Is that why you came here?" he asked, keeping his voice quiet and soft. But when she turned her soft brown eyes to his, he reached up to touch her chin without even realizing he was doing so.

Her pupils dilated at his touch. Kane swallowed hard. "Tell me, Annie. Who hurt you?"

THREE

He watched her pulse vibrate the tender skin below her ear, then he dragged his gaze to hers, willing her to answer him with his eyes.

"No one. I came here to get away."

"From what? Who?"

She looked into his eyes for what seemed an eternity. Her lashes drifted shut for several seconds, and Kane knew then that he had lost. She wasn't going to tell him what had happened. Not yet.

She opened her eyes and said, "No one. I just wanted to be alone for a while."

Kane let his fingers drift up along her jaw and tuck a wayward wild red curl behind her ear. "Okay," he said finally. "But can I ask you to do one thing for me?"

He let his hand drop when she leaned away from his touch.

"That depends."

"When you decide you can trust me, will you tell me what really happened?"

"But noth—"

Kane stopped her denial by placing one finger across her lips. "Just don't lie to me."

She stepped back so they were no longer touching, staring at him as if uncertain whether to break down and confess—or run hard in the opposite direction.

She did neither, nor did she answer him. She simply walked away. She'd gone about ten feet when she turned back to him. "What makes you think someone hurt me?"

Kane realized he was in trouble. He couldn't tell her who he was. Who had sent him. Shouldn't want to. But for the first time in his life, he found himself questioning his motives. What bothered him even more was the fact that no matter how much he hated the unsettling emotions she raised in him, he knew he couldn't come right out and lie to her. Not at this moment. So he told her what he could.

"My Shoshone name is 'Eyes of the Hawk.' It was given to me at age twelve by a tribal elder. One of the children had wandered off and become lost. Everyone looked for her for hours. I happened to spot her tracks."

"How did you know they were hers?"

"I knew that Lucy always dragged her stuffed dog around with her. I noticed small tracks leaving the playground with a drag mark in the dirt between the footprints. I followed it and eventually found her hiding beneath a porch. She'd hidden because she'd torn her dress and thought she'd get in trouble."

"What does that have to do with me?"

"I was given the name because I notice things others don't. Small things most people take for granted or are too busy to see."

He could tell she hesitated over her next question, and he willed her to ask it.

"What do you see when you look at me?"

He walked to stand directly in front of her, but didn't touch her. He waited until she lifted her gaze to his. "I see a woman who needs to be with others. A woman who may *need* to be alone, but doesn't *want* to be alone."

A long moment elapsed before she answered him. "You may be right, Eyes of the Hawk," she said in a whisper. "But I don't want to talk about it. Okay?"

Kane's muscles tightened with need. The need to kiss her, to taste her pain and her strength, to forge a bond with her that was as physical as it was mental. When she'd spoken his Shoshone name, it had moved something deep within him.

It shook him so badly, he didn't dare to so much as touch her. Breathing in her scent was almost more than he could stand.

"Just know," he said, his usually even voice rough with need, "that I am here when you do."

She dipped her chin in the barest of nods.

Kane watched her as she turned and walked

away. Her dyed red hair with its sexy unnatural curl, her squared slender shoulders that carried an unknown burden, a waist made for big hands like his to grip, hips that would cushion the need that strained hard against the zipper of his jeans, strong legs that would hold him tightly in place.

And more than anything in the world, at that moment, he wished Sam Perkins dead.

Not only because he was convinced the man had wronged his wife in some way, but because only then would she be free to come to him.

He tilted his head to look heavenward. "I am a fool." He dropped his chin. "I'm also no saint," he muttered, wondering if the Fates were finally punishing him for his many faults, as Cloud Dancer had said countless times they would. Only he'd never imagined his penance would come in the form of a woman he could need more than want, but never have.

Elizabeth wiped her forehead with a corner of the old sheet she'd torn and wrapped around her waist as an apron. The steam rising from the pot in front of her wasn't the only reason for her heated condition. She'd spent over an hour in the fields that morning, then worked in the kitchen all afternoon. And not a minute had passed that she'd been able to think of anything except Kane Hawthorne and what had happened between them.

There was no denying the effect his dark sensuality and quiet, purposeful demeanor had on her equilibrium. But even more disturbing was the idea of just how special a man he might be. He struck her as honest and caring.

But then, hadn't she once thought the same things of Sam Perkins?

The hair on her neck stood up even though damp with perspiration. Yeah. She was one hell of a judge of character all right. Theirs hadn't been the passion of a lifetime—Sam was a bit too conservative for that sort of behavior—but for a secretary working to make ends meet, having a whirlwind courtship with a bank president she'd met at a church social was pretty heady stuff. And when he'd asked her to marry him mere months later, she hadn't hesitated to say yes. After all, what more could she have wanted? She knew many women would have killed to have been in her position.

Now the only one who wanted to do the killing was Sam.

"I never should have followed him that night," she whispered into the steamy room. It wasn't the first time she'd uttered that sentiment. Unfortunately that didn't change anything. How wrong she'd been to think Sam was perfect for her. So incredibly, horribly wrong.

She thought back to that morning. To the secret thrill that had raced through her when Kane had touched her lips with his rough-tipped finger.

No. She knew enough, had learned enough about herself over these past few months to realize how vulnerable she was. Because he seemed to care wasn't a good enough reason to give in to the overwhelming urge to unburden herself and share her problems.

Besides, if he was as decent as he seemed, he certainly didn't need to have his honest work rewarded with being embroiled in her potentially dangerous situation.

But you've already involved him, a little voice nagged.

"Does that forlorn face mean you won't have time for dinner?"

She started badly, then had to laugh as she turned. It felt good. Seeing him in her doorway, even sweaty and tired, made her feel better. "I guess I'll have to get used to jumping every time we begin a conversation."

His lips curved a bit, and her heart skipped several beats at the change the small smile made in his harsh features.

"At least this time I didn't cost you a day's work. I'll try to make more noise in the future."

Future. A word she'd always taken for granted. It held such potential—for everyone but her. Elizabeth caught his gaze on her and quickly turned back to stir the jam she was making. Eyes of the Hawk. A very appropriate name.

"Thanks," she mumbled. Then recalling his question, she said, "I'm sorry, but I haven't fixed anything to eat. I'm using both burners to cook down some jam. It'll probably be another hour."

She didn't add that she had no idea what she was going to cook. Stew, salad, and rolls was her basic menu.

"Actually, that works out fine. I thought I'd wash up in the spring behind the barn. Then maybe see if I could find a way to contribute to the dinner menu. You wouldn't happen to have a fishing pole, would you?"

"I doubt you'd catch anything in the spring."

He shook his head. "I noticed that stream about a half mile down the road as I rode in yesterday."

She smiled, touched at his attempt to ease her load. "Unfortunately, I don't remember seeing any poles. At least not that I've found. Maybe in the shed?"

"No. I've been all through that."

"Not surprising I guess. I can't picture Grandma Fielding reeling one in."

"What about her granddaughter?"

She looked up at him. "You mean, do I fish?"

"Is that such a strange question?"

"Not really, I guess. I did as a child, with Matt and my dad. But it's been a long time." She shrugged off the wistfulness that threatened every time she thought of her brother. "I don't see what difference it makes, since we don't have poles."

"Some obstacles are easier to overcome than others," he answered quietly. "When you get done, why don't you pack some of your rolls and jam and meet me by the creek? Take your truck so you don't have to hike it. I'll leave Sky Dancer tied where you can see her."

"I don't mind the walk, but how are you—?"

"Trust has to start somewhere, Annie," he broke in. "You provided dinner last night. Tonight it's on me. Deal?"

Ann. She'd always hated her middle name. It was so plain. Annie was even worse. At least she used to think so.

"If it will make you feel any better, we can discuss the repairs I want to make in here while we eat."

His crooked smile returned, melting away any remaining resistance she had left. It wasn't as if they hadn't eaten together before. "Yeah," she said with a smile, "we have a deal."

He nodded and was gone.

"What in the hell do you think you're doing, Hawthorne," he asked himself. He strode to the bunkhouse and gathered a change of clothes. At the door he cursed, turned, and grabbed the small leather kit from his saddlebag. He didn't even try to rationalize why he was going to shave.

He pulled himself onto the Appaloosa's bare back and rode behind the house and down the rutted dirt road toward the weather-beaten Lazy F sign. He decided to forgo the spring. He could save time by bathing at the stream. Then maybe by the time she arrived, he'd have his act together. Tonight was a perfect opportunity to get some answers from her. He simply needed a plan.

An immediate, very pleasurable idea sprang to mind, as well as to another part of his anatomy. But, as appealing and intensely satisfying as the result would likely be, he could not consider seduction. He laughed at himself. What an ego. She may look at him with those soft doe eyes of hers and make him think of long afternoons spent lazily exploring each other's bodies. But if her married status was enough of an obstacle to prevent him from trying to seduce her, what made him think her vows didn't hold the same importance to her?

In all his struggling to come to grips with his response to her, he'd never once wondered about her response to him.

Had she given any indication that she'd ignore her marriage vows even in lieu of some trouble—no matter how disturbing the reason—in her marriage to Sam? No. The woman he'd observed and spoken to in the last forty-eight hours was a woman of pride and integrity. He'd stake his fee on it.

Kane tugged at the bandanna tied at his neck and pressed his heels against the mare's flanks, easing her into a canter. The jarring motion as they covered the uneven ground did little to shake free the vague, unsettling notion that Annie didn't *feel* like a married woman to him.

"Kane?"

He froze for an instant. Damn, he hadn't even heard her approach. What was wrong with him? He tugged his jeans quickly over his hips. The zipper took a few seconds longer. That was what was wrong with him. And if the freezing creek water hadn't cured it, nothing would.

"Over here." He shook the water from his hair, raking it back with one hand while grabbing for his shirt with the other.

"This looks wonderful."

Kane brushed past the trees and entered the clearing. Annie was standing by the small fire he'd made and was admiring the grate he'd fashioned from a piece of old wire fencing. "No big deal," he said honestly. "It'll look a lot better when there's a few fish cooking on it."

"Matthew would have loved to have had a friend like you as a child. He almost flunked Eagle Scouts . . ." She turned to face him as she spoke, but whatever she'd been about to say was apparently forgotten as she stared at him.

He looked down at himself, wondering belatedly if his condition by the stream was still so apparent that he'd embarrassed her. But all he saw was his wet chest and damp jeans, the shirt still in his hands hanging in front of him. He glanced back up at her with a questioning look.

"I, uh . . ." She laughed a bit nervously and turned back to the fire.

"What?" He walked toward her as he spoke.

She didn't turn to face him. "I feel stupid, is what." She took an audible breath and looked over at him, a self-deprecating smile curved her lips. "Don't take this the wrong way, it's just that you . . . you look . . ." Again, her voice drifted off and she turned back to the fire.

Ignoring all the reasons he shouldn't, he touched her shoulder, urging her to gaze at him. She did. "I'm sorry if I embarrassed you. I stayed in the stream a bit longer than I thought." He didn't add that she would have been a helluva lot more embarrassed if he hadn't. He lifted his hand and slipped on his shirt. He quickly fastened the buttons of the faded red cotton favorite, then held his arms out wide. "Is that better?"

"Yes. I mean, you were fine . . . really . . . fine, before." She looked away. "I don't know why I'm acting like such an idiot."

Thinking of his own feelings, he seconded the notion. Especially as he heard himself ask, "Would you prefer I leave it off?"

Her head whipped around. "No! That is, listen, I'm starving. Why don't we try and catch dinner?"

He hid his smile at her too-quick response. Starving. So was he. And fish was the farthest thing from his mind. He'd wondered earlier about her reaction to him. Not that he'd staged this little scene to find out, but he couldn't argue that the results had been . . . stimulating. He frowned. "Yeah, dinner. Maybe that's not a bad idea."

She walked across the clearing, strolled almost,

then turned to face him once she was safely on the other side of the fire. "So, Eyes of the Hawk," she asked with a bright smile, "how do we catch them? With our bare hands?"

"We could."

She stared at him for a moment, apparently trying to determine if he was serious. She went on before he could elaborate.

"Correction. *You* could. I didn't excel in eye-hand coordination skills in school. And I have to admit I'm not too partial to standing in freezing water while I practice, either. How about you catch, I cook?"

He couldn't recall having the desire to smile so often in a long while. Elizabeth Ann—though he already found himself thinking of her as Annie—may be taken, but there was no law that said he couldn't enjoy her company.

"I said, we *could*. But I was planning on a more traditional approach." He walked over to a tall larch closer to the water's edge and lifted two slender branches that had been leaning against the trunk. He'd tied some fine string to the end of each one and fashioned hooks from two pieces of wire.

He motioned her to follow him as he turned and headed up the bank a few yards. "I found a likely spot up here," he called over his shoulder. "Biggest catch cooks, smallest cleans the fish."

He hoisted himself up on a rock and baited their hooks. She caught up to him a second later and after a brief hesitation, scooted onto the spot next to him.

She smelled like preserves. He'd detected the sweet scent earlier, by the fire, but thought it was the jam in the basket she'd carried. His mouth watered, and he deliberately turned his head away.

She plopped her line into the water. "You'd better hope I catch a monster, because I've never cooked a fish that can still stare at me."

Kane gave in to the urge to smile. They sat in silence for a while, each had had a few nibbles, but no luck so far. Kane's stomach was growling, he was tired and frustrated with his indecision about what he was going to do with her. Just then she got another tug, and with a yank, a fish flopped on top of the water. She turned a triumphant smile on Kane, and suddenly he was having the time of his life.

"Careful, or you'll pull the hook right out of him," he cautioned.

Not listening to him, too caught up in her little drama, she alternately yanked and pulled the rod one way then the other. Finally, on a frustrated growl she whipped the pole back, and the fish literally flew out of the water.

It landed directly in his lap.

She gasped. "I'm sorry!"

Kane jumped and would have scrambled to his feet had Annie not instinctively dived after the slippery trout.

"Sit still so I can get a hold on him," she instructed as she grappled with the elusive fish.

Kane gritted his teeth as her hands grappled with him as well. "Annie, stop."

"If you'd just—"

He caught her wrists in a tight grip. "I'll get the fish. It's not as if it's going to do any damage." He had pulled her against his chest, and she lay sprawled half in his lap. He couldn't seem to tear his gaze away from her.

"I'm sorry," she said at length. The fish slapped against his thigh with an audible thwack, and she blushed. "I told you my eye-hand coordination stunk."

Kane grabbed the fish, biting down hard on the urge to tell her that her hands had been doing just fine. And as for those soft brown eyes . . . And those lips . . . He began lowering his head to hers before he even realized his intention.

"Kane?"

"Mmm?" he whispered, more intrigued by the breathy quality of her voice as she said his name, then what her use of it implied. He inhaled her scent as her lips parted on a sigh. He lifted his hand to cup her head and was yanked back to reality when the fish he'd been holding in it slipped to the rock and began flopping.

Annie tumbled from his lap as they both reached for the squirming fish.

"I got it." Kane grunted as he twisted back to a sitting position, tightening his grip on the fish and his still-rocketing hormones. "Nice catch," he grumbled, then made himself turn to look at her. She had righted herself, but her hair was sticking out at odd angles, her cheeks were flushed, and her brown eyes had never been so bright. He smiled. "Even if your form is original."

Her blush deepened, but she managed to smile. "Hey, don't knock it. At least I caught one."

If asked, he couldn't have said what made him do it. The challenge in her eyes? Or maybe it was the need to immerse some part of his body in cold water again before he did something really stupid—such as kiss her sweet, wisecracking mouth until neither one of them cared about marriage vows and ugly pasts.

When he realized that idea turned him on more than it bothered him, he swiftly bent to roll up his jeans' legs, then waded into the stream. It took considerable control not to suck in his breath. Even in July, streams close to the Canadian border remained frigid. He motioned for her to be quiet by placing a finger across his lips.

He turned away when she adopted a "Who me?" look then composed her face into the picture of serious contemplation. Enjoying her company was one thing, but he hoped he had enough brains left to realize that letting her know how much he did wasn't going to help either one of them when he took her back to Boise.

That thought managed to do what the cold water hadn't, and he shut off his mind completely and concentrated on the task at hand.

❖───────❖

He plunged his hands into the frigid stream for the third time and finally captured his prey. "Good thing," he muttered under his breath as he yanked the fish up and hooked his numbed fingers in the gills. His toes had lost all feeling about ten minutes earlier, and he didn't think he had a fourth try in him.

He waded ashore and tossed the fish in the bucket beside Annie.

"Wow! How'd you do that? I've heard of people catching fish with their bare hands, but I've never actually seen it. Mrs. Wadlow would have loved you."

"Who's Mrs. Wadlow?"

"My first grade teacher. That woman made it her mission in life to get me to be able to play a simple game of jacks."

"Did she succeed?"

"I'll put it this way; thank goodness jack skills aren't required learning for secretarial school."

Kane lifted the bucket and held out his hand. She stared at it for a moment before reaching for it.

Her hand was a lot smaller than his, and he remembered how slim her wrists had been when he'd grabbed them. The fragility implied in that was directly at odds with the rough calluses that briefly scraped his palm before she let go. *Why have you done this to yourself?* he wanted to ask. He resisted the urge to curl his fingers into a fist, as if he could hold the feel of her there.

They'd gone several steps when he asked, "Is

that what you were before coming here?" At her blank look, he said, "A secretary, I mean."

"Oh, that. Yes, I was."

"You plan on going back to it?"

They were close to the clearing before she answered. He wondered if she was really undecided or simply not certain whether to trust him.

"I'm not sure what I'm going to do when I leave here."

Kane knew she spoke the truth. "I guess if you're going to the trouble to expand your jams and preserves operation, you must be planning to stay here for a while."

She cast a quick glance at him as they crossed the clearing to the fire, which had burned down to glowing embers. "At least until my brother comes back from overseas."

Kane tensed at the unexpected answer but quickly willed himself to relax. He knew from his research that Matthew Lawson was out of the country on some sort of job for the government, which Annie had corroborated the day before. He also knew she hadn't left him a note of any kind. He'd found a small safe in the back bedroom, but it had been empty. He doubted it had been that way when Annie arrived. There had been no activity on her personal accounts at Sam's bank, nor on any of her three credit cards. She hadn't come this far north and lived for several months on jam money.

"You said you didn't see him often. When do you expect him? The holidays?" Kane kept the questions casual, hoping she'd take them as typical get-to-know-you interest.

"Sooner, I hope," she said, her tone undeniably fervent. "I really miss him."

Before he could frame the next question, she turned to him and asked, "How about you? You said you left Fort Hall as a teenager. Do you ever see your family?"

He should have expected the question, but he hadn't. Maybe because she seemed so sincere. It had been a very long time since anyone had expressed enough interest in him to ask about his personal life. That realization didn't disturb him half as much as discovering he didn't mind answering her.

"No. I have no contact with my family."

"You never went back, did you?" Her voice was even, with no trace of pity or censure.

"Once."

She waited for him to continue.

"My grandmother died about ten years ago. I was in my early twenties then. I went back when I heard."

He squatted by the fire and concentrated on filleting the fish and arranging them on the makeshift grill.

"But you didn't stay."

"No. Cloud Dancer had spent many years trying to instill in me the pride of my people, my heritage. I resented it then."

"But you understand it better now."

He looked up at her, locking his gaze on hers.

There was so much wisdom in those deep brown eyes. "Yes."

She held his gaze until the snapping of the fire made him turn his attention back to the fish. Out of the corner of his eyes, he watched her retrieve the jam and biscuits along with the blanket she'd brought, and set about arranging them under the larches by the water.

He breathed a small sigh of relief that she'd let the topic drop. After all, he was there to get information out of her. Not the other way around.

Once the fish were cooking, he brushed his hands and moved to stand.

"You seem very proud of your Native American heritage," she began.

He stilled for a moment, then continued to stretch into a standing position. "I am."

"Why did you leave the first time? I guess it's just that I miss my brother and can't understand why anyone would willingly leave such a special part of himself behind."

He walked over to the blanket, his tall form casting a shadow over her. In a quiet, even voice he said, "Maybe it wasn't so special when I left."

She held his gaze. "And now?"

He sighed. The woman was nothing if not tenacious. "And now my family is gone. There is nothing for me there."

She curled onto her knees and started to reach out to touch his leg, then checked the motion. She settled back on her heels instead. "I shouldn't have asked. I won't bring it up again."

He was surprised at how disappointed he was that she hadn't touched him. He could almost feel her small callused hand on him, on his leg, higher . . .

He growled and swung around, stalking back to the fire. "The fish will be ready in a few minutes." He kept his back to her and needlessly poked at the embers with a long stick.

"I'm glad you're here, Kane Hawthorne."

Kane hung his head and softly swore every curse he knew in the English language, then switched to his native tongue and exhausted those too. "I wish I could say the same, sweet Annie," he said under his breath. "I wish to hell I could say the same."

FOUR

Elizabeth packed the last two jars of preserves in the cardboard box, then hefted it to one hip, using the other one to bump the screen door open. After placing it in the back of the pickup along with the other two boxes, she took a moment to wipe her forehead on the sleeve of her berry-stained yellow T-shirt.

She stepped onto the front porch, a smile crossing her face again as she looked at the newly straightened railing. Kane had repaired it that morning. Right after he'd fixed the legs on the kitchen table. She pushed through the small front room on into the kitchen, thinking about their conversation over the freshly cooked fish last evening.

After the intense moment by the stream, followed by the even more intense conversation about Kane's past, he'd kept the dinner conversation strictly business. She'd spent most of the rest of the night trying to convince herself she was relieved.

Kane had told her that by recycling the unused materials from the barn and bunkhouse renovation, he could fix quite a bit. A lot more than she'd planned on. She knew she should have told him she didn't intend to stay long enough to make some of the repairs necessary. But the memory of the kiss they'd almost shared made her unwilling to ruin the remainder of their outing with a lot of unwanted questions.

She pushed out the back door, glancing up as she always did at the stunning view of the Selkirk Mountains. She wondered if, given the right circumstances, she might enjoy living out there. A loud bang followed by what sounded like swearing jerked her from her thoughts.

She headed for the barn, a smile curving her lips as she concentrated on the loudly spoken language with a strange flat intonation. Whatever it was, it wasn't English.

Intrigued, she quietly ducked inside the opening where the warped barn doors used to hang. She found Kane gripping one hand with the other, glaring at his open palm. She was a step away when he looked up.

"Don't just stand there," he demanded, "grab a pair of pliers."

Caught off guard, she stopped short. "Pliers? What did you do that requires pliers?" she asked, concerned that he'd really hurt himself. "Here, let me see."

She reached for his hand and tugged gently until

she had his large callused hand cradled in her palms. His skin was dusty and very warm. She told herself her fingers trembled slightly because she was concerned about his apparent wound, not because she could feel his breath fan against her cheek as she angled his hand to catch a ray of sunlight.

It took a second, but she found it. She forced herself not to smile, but he must have seen the muscles in her jaw twitch, because he pulled his hand away.

"No big deal, I'll take care of it," he said gruffly.

"I'll find the pliers," she said solemnly. "Maybe I should get the saw in case we need to amputate." He shot her a look that should have reduced her and the barn to ashes. She didn't flinch. Allowing her lips to curve slightly, she said, "Hey, you don't need to explain the dangers to me. If that splinter got infected, you could lose the whole arm."

He spun around and walked up to her until there was barely a breath of air between them. She faced his flinty expression as squarely as she could given the difference in their heights. There must be a reason why she shouldn't be having fun with him, she thought absently, but for the life of her, she couldn't think of what it could be.

He grabbed her left arm, raising it beside them until the Band-Aid on her forearm was level with her eyes. "For someone who howled like a stuck pig this morning over a puny steam burn, you sure are having a good laugh."

She gasped. "Hey, having a patch of your skin

bubble up and slide off your arm is worth a good scream. And I did not sound like a pig," she added as an afterthought.

Her gaze shifted to his hand, then to his stormy eyes.

"Does it still hurt?" he asked after a long moment.

She shook her head, wondering where her voice had gone. His thumb rubbed over the edges of her bandage as he continued to stare. She felt trapped by his dark eyes, but couldn't deny the bond excited her as much as they disturbed her. Her breathing came out in little gasps.

"You sure?"

"Yeah," she managed, her voice hoarse. "Yours needs tending to, though. Let me see this." She pulled his hand up between them. "It's not too bad, but it has to come out."

He bent over, placing his lips near her ear. "There was always one remedy I wanted to try."

She didn't dare look up. Just the heat of his breath on her skin was making her toes curl. She hated danger. Had spent three hideous months hiding from it. So why was she willingly courting it now by not moving away from him?

"Which one is that?" she heard herself ask.

"The one about kissing it to make it better."

She thought about running while she still could, but that impulse died when she looked into his eyes. Something she saw there, past the teasing, past the sensual wordplay, tugged at her in a deep, dark place she hadn't examined since her parents had died. "No one ever did that for you?"

"Never let anyone try."

The tugging sensation became a clutch near her heart. Purposely ignoring conscious thought, she drew his hand up to her face. She closed her eyes and pressed a soft kiss to the warm skin beside the small wound.

A soft groan escaped him, and her eyes opened as she looked up to him. "Did I hurt you?"

He stared at her for so long, she decided he wasn't going to answer her. Then he pulled his hand gently from her grasp and said, "Thank you."

Before she could ask him to explain, he stepped away and moved over to the toolbox, rummaging through it before speaking again. "Was there some reason you came out here?"

His tone was flat, but he wasn't angry. At least she didn't think so. She didn't know what to think. He had her emotions running in circles so tight, she felt almost strangled by them. Deciding maybe it was best to follow his lead, she answered his question. "Actually, I came out here to tell you I was going down to Boundary Gap to deliver a batch of jam to Dobs."

Kane's head whipped up.

Elizabeth was caught off guard by the sudden intensity of his gaze as he stared at her for a moment. This time there was no sensual promise, or deeply hidden wounds. His expression was alert and focused, almost like a predator who's scented his prey.

She waited for him to say something, but he apparently decided against it, because he resumed his search through the toolbox.

Feeling a sudden need for fresh air and wide open spaces, she turned to go. "You need anything?"

"Yeah," he answered without looking up, "the needle nose pliers."

"Oh, for heaven's sake. Wait here a minute." Exasperated now by his obvious intention to return to his taciturn self, she headed for the door. The sooner she fixed his damn hand, the sooner she could get out for a much-needed break. She was two steps from the door when he spoke again.

"Never mind."

She turned in time to see him pull a very lethal looking knife from the sheath she'd noticed he always had strapped on his belt. He'd turned it so he could use the pointed tip on his palm before she broke out of her momentary shock.

"Hey! Don't do that!" She hurried across the hard-packed dirt floor to the makeshift bench where he was seated.

The deadly looking blade a hairbreadth away from his flesh, he looked up at her, his expression unconcerned. "You were the one telling me about the horrors of infection."

"I may live out in the boonies, but I do have

enough sense to have a first-aid kit. Come up to the house and let me take that sliver out the right way."

In one clean motion, he slid the blade smoothly in its leather sheath, tossed the pliers back into the box, and stood. "Well, why didn't you say so?"

Grumbling under her breath about men in general and Kane in particular, she turned and stalked out the door.

She was halfway across the yard when he said, "And it's not a sliver, it's a chunk."

Despite attempts to stifle it, his petulant remark brought a smile to her lips. Damn the man for always managing to catch her off guard. She entered the kitchen and motioned to the table. "Have a seat, I'll be right back."

Kane felt like an idiot sitting at the tiny kitchen table, waiting like some kid for Mom to come take care of his boo-boo. He didn't know what had prompted his kiss-it-and-make-it-better proposal out in the barn. It had been foolish, not to mention dangerous. Her sweet, healing kiss had taken him completely off guard.

He didn't think he'd ever forget how she'd looked at him or how when her thick lashes had drifted over her newly tanned cheeks, he'd felt his heart drop to his knees. "Damn freckles," he muttered.

He forced himself to stop visualizing those tantalizing little brown spots that splashed so provocatively across the bridge of her cute little nose—as if she'd purposely placed each and every one of them with the intention of driving him crazy—and turned his mind to her proposed outing today.

He knew from talking with her over dinner that she only went down into the tiny mountain town once a week, but that didn't soothe his instincts. The idea of her traveling over that lonely stretch of mountain road in her rusty excuse for a truck bothered him more than he wanted to admit. He knew his concern was only partly based on the probability that the guy tailing him when he left Boise might have picked up his trail after he'd ditched him in Coeur d'Alene.

"This whole thing stinks to high heaven," he said as he studied the small room, thinking again that she was damn lucky the old house hadn't caved in on her head while she slept. A good high wind . . .

"Are you still grumbling over that tiny fleck of wood?"

He turned his attention to the doorway and had to fight the surprising urge to smile. She was dressed in old jeans—sans the sponges—and a canary-yellow T-shirt that sported berry stains in excruciatingly tempting places. No, he didn't want her to mother him.

What he wanted was for her to come closer so he could remove those berry stains—with his tongue.

He shifted in his seat and looked at his hand as she dumped her supplies on the table.

Scooting her chair to face his, she pulled his hand into her lap. The instant his knuckles brushed her denim-covered thigh, he pulled it right back.

"Just shove that stuff over where I can reach it, I can take it from here." His tone was gruffer than necessary, but what the heck. She was lucky he didn't wipe the table clean and haul her on top of it instead.

"Really, Kane—"

"Really, Annie," he shot back, and reached for the pair of tweezers she'd laid next to the alcohol.

With a sigh of defeat, she shoved her chair back and stood. She started to leave the room when he finally looked up. "You sure that truck will make it to Boundary Gap and back?"

She turned around, a look of surprise on her face. Apparently he hadn't sounded as casual as he'd intended.

"It's made it so far. I know it looks bad, but it runs okay."

She shrugged a bit self-consciously, and he felt his chest tighten even further. He knew what she'd been driving when she'd left Sam and Boise behind three months earlier. That sleek blue BMW was a damn sight more luxurious than a battered pickup with a questionable heritage. "Would you mind some company?"

"Ah, y-yeah . . . sure," she stammered. She glanced down and, as if noting for the first time the big red blotches covering selective patches of her shirt, she said, "I'll be right back."

Kane didn't bother swallowing his smile this time. He turned his attention back to the operation he was performing on his hand, which was more than a little tricky given it was in his left palm and he was left-handed. A minor detail he'd rather cut off his hand than admit to her at this point. She was really something. His grin didn't fade, even when he eventually tossed the useless tweezers back on the table and pulled the knife out again.

He was already in the truck, motor running, when she pushed through the torn screen door.

She leaned in the passenger window. "You don't have to drive."

"I don't mind." His right hand held the steering wheel. His left was tucked out of sight.

She looked at him uncertainly for a moment. He was about to reassure her he could handle her precious truck, when she shrugged and walked around the back and up to his window.

"Okay, but you'll have to get out to let me in. The passenger door doesn't work."

He rolled his eyes. "Don't you own anything that isn't a step away from disintegrating?" He wasn't prepared for the flash of pain that crossed her face.

"Aw, hell," he muttered, and without thinking yanked the door open with his left hand. The pain was so severe, he didn't remember to curse in Shoshone.

Annie yanked open the door and grabbed his hand while he was still swearing. "What did you do, Hawthorne?"

"Nothing." He clenched the hand in question into a fist to keep her from seeing his impromptu surgery.

She didn't even bother arguing with him this time.

"Move over," she ordered. "I'm driving."

She was altogether too cute when she got mad. He almost said "Yes, ma'am" just for the reaction he'd likely get, but he bit his tongue and shifted around the gear stick to the other side.

She hopped in and slammed the door. Tossing a glance out the rear window, she threw the truck in reverse and backed out in a cloud of dust.

They'd traveled for several bone-jarring minutes when he said, "You drive this rust trap pretty well for a secretary."

She shot him a quick glance before turning her attention back to the rutted lane that served as a road. "And you crawled over that gear shift pretty gracefully for someone who needs major medical coverage for a simple splinter removal."

Kane let out a surprised bark of laughter which distracted her. "Look out," he cautioned as they headed for a sloping curve, "all the sweet kisses in the world won't put me back together if you drive this thing over the edge."

He watched the flush climb into her cheeks as she quickly turned her attention to the road. He was half tempted to ask her to pull over so he could find out how easily the rest of her body blushed. He shifted in his seat.

"You should do that more often, you know?" she said after a lengthy silence.

It took him a moment to realize she meant his short burst of laughter. She was probably right. But he usually didn't have much to laugh about. He ignored the twinge in the center of his chest and turned back to her. "Maybe you should take your own advice," he suggested quietly. He was glad for the pain in his left hand. It was the only thing that kept him from reaching out and running his fingers down the side of her face. "I bet you used to laugh all the time."

The tightened jawline and sudden working of the muscles in her throat gave him his answer.

"Why are you really here, Annie? What made you run?"

Her whole body stiffened. Her knuckles on the steering wheel were pure white. "What makes you think I'm running?"

"A woman like you doesn't send herself into self-imposed exile in one of the harshest landscapes in the country because she needs a little break."

"A woman like me?" Elizabeth queried softly, almost more to herself than to Kane. "What do you know of women like me?"

Elizabeth sensed the complete stillness inside the truck. It belatedly occurred to her that he had taken her comment the wrong way. She'd reached a flat stretch of road with a wider than usual shoulder. She immediately slowed the truck and pulled over, then shoved the gear shift into neutral and turned her attention to him.

She froze. The words she'd been about to say lodged hard in her throat. She had his complete attention. And with a man as intense as Kane Hawthorne, it was a palpable thing. His eyes glittered, black and shiny. His lips, which she'd found herself staring at more than once, were compressed into a flat, emotionless line.

She wanted to reach out for him. To him. Something in the fierce pride that literally shouted from every rigidly held muscle in his body made her want to pull him into her arms and hold on tight.

"Kane, that comment was self-directed. If you think for one minute that your heritage . . ." She let her words drift as the irony of what she was doing hit her. She'd spent the last three months in hiding from a man whose beliefs were so opposite hers, she'd put her very life in jeopardy to try and change his mind. And now she was having to convince Kane she wasn't prejudiced. If he only knew.

The sudden urge to tell him everything was so overwhelming, she gripped the door handle, intending to jump out for a quick dose of fresh air and common sense.

"Annie, stop." He didn't reach for her, but the power of his voice held her still just as effectively. "I know you didn't mean it that way. I'm sorry."

"I take it you've encountered the attitude once or twice."

"You could say that."

Without thinking, she shifted a bit closer. "Well, you can bet the ranch that I don't have a bigoted bone in my body," she said fervently. On a roll, she added, "As a matter of fact, your Shoshone heritage intrigues me quite a bit."

She'd been looking him square in the face, wanting to leave no doubt as to her sincerity. So it was impossible to miss the sudden change in his dark eyes. The glitter was still there, but it wasn't heated now. Well, yes it was. But with an entirely different flame as its source.

"*Da'bEntcotc*," he intoned softly, "don't look too deep inside me. My *mu'gua* is too black for the likes of you."

The odd rhythm of his words wafted through her mind like the soft musical sound of water rushing over rocks. "What did that mean?"

"*Mu'gua* means soul."

"And the other?"

He turned abruptly to face the windshield. "Shouldn't we be getting into town? You don't want to drive these roads in the dark."

Elizabeth wanted to press him for an answer, but she let it go. For now. For good, if she was smart. She knew it was dangerous to get any further involved with Kane than she already was. He was an employee of sorts, nothing more. But she couldn't deny the attraction she felt. With a look or a quiet word, he managed to touch her on levels she hadn't been aware she'd possessed.

She shifted into first and steered onto the road, studiously avoiding looking at Kane even in her peripheral vision. But she kept hearing the words he'd spoken.

She pulled into the gravel parking lot that fronted Dobs's country store and the Boundary Gap post office. Still a bit unsettled, she hopped down without glancing at Kane.

She was forced to when they both reached for the tailgate at the same time. "Thanks," she said quietly when he popped the bent handle to lower the gate down, glad she sounded calm and casual. Remembering his hand, she said, "Maybe you'd better let me get these."

In answer, Kane pulled two of the boxes to the edge, stacked one on the other, and hefted them to his right hip. "These go to Dobs, right?"

She didn't bother to argue with him. "I'll get the other two and meet you inside." He dipped his chin in a brief nod and moved toward the wooden steps leading up to the screen door, which was propped open with an old cola crate. "Stubborn as a mule," she muttered, ignoring the fact that she'd have been disappointed if he'd reacted any differently.

She struggled to stack the boxes, the cardboard not being too sturdy. She had to use both arms to carry them, but she managed to get up the stairs in time to catch the tail end of a conversation between Dobs and Kane.

"Glad to hear she had enough smarts to take on some help," Dobs was saying. "Didn't much care for the idea of a little thing like her on that deserted patch of land all by herself."

"You have much trouble around here?" Kane asked.

Elizabeth paused on the second-to-last step, telling herself it was to catch her breath. Kane's question had been casual. Too casual? She waited for Dobs's reply.

"Naw, no more than the occasional unlicensed hunter or rowdy farmhand with too much payday and too little sense."

"I understand the Lazy F has been abandoned for a long time. Guess it's natural you'd be concerned."

Elizabeth shifted the boxes in her arms, trying to keep the glass jars from chinking together. Kane wasn't the type to make useless small talk. Even after knowing him for only a few days, she realized there had to be a reason for his comments. She thought about the reference list he'd given her, which she'd stuck in her pocket before leaving the house earlier. Only now it was a bit harder to deny that her reasons for wanting to contact the names on the list were strictly business related.

She hefted her load up the last step and walked into the store. "Hi, Dobs, hope you got enough room to store these for a few days till Ms. Wentland stops back over."

She smiled at the grizzled old man, the warmth in her voice sincere. He was barely a hair over five feet, almost as round as he was tall, with a ring of shocking white hair crowning his otherwise bald head. She'd wondered when she'd first seen him if he'd compensated for the lack of hair on top by growing his beard to St. Nicholas proportions. But she knew now it had nothing to do with vanity. He was a sharp businessman who'd sustained his tiny store for almost fifty years and owed his success—to hear him tell it, as she had more than once—to plain speaking, faith in the good Lord above, and a healthy respect for homemade whiskey.

Kane stepped forward and relieved her of her burden, carefully placing the boxes on the scarred linoleum counter next to the others he'd carried in.

"No problem, Miz Fielding. I got plenty of room. Looks like you outdone yourself. Miz Wentland will be pleased." He tipped up on his toes and rummaged through one of the boxes. "Wouldn't happen to have any raspberry jam this time around?"

Elizabeth's smile broadened. "Hold on." She dashed out to the truck and lifted the canvas tote she'd stashed by the wheel hub. She hopped up the stairs and back into the cool store. "Here you go," she said, pulling two mason jars from the tan bag. "Special for you."

Kane hid his surprise as the old man blushed at

Annie's offering. *So, she even gets to old busybodies,* he thought wryly. He was glad for Dobs's penchant for sticking his nose in everyone's business, it made him a perfect source for information. Looking at him now, though, his cheeks even ruddier than usual as he accepted the jars and turned to go stash them in the back room, Kane imagined that not too many people stuck their nose in Dobs's business.

He turned his attention back to Annie, who was pulling a list out of her jeans' pocket.

"I need to get some feed for Sky Dancer."

"There's a feed store at the bottom of the mountain—"

"No, I'll make do with what he has here. I want to supplement her diet so she doesn't graze down your grass too badly. I'd like to get a bale or two of hay as well, if you have enough room in the back of the truck."

"No problem. I have a package at the post office, but it should be small."

He forced his tone to remain light. "Mail day, huh? More jars?"

She smiled, and Kane silently damned himself for having to probe each facet of her life under the guise of friendship. It would be so nice if he could just . . . *what, Hawthorne?* Let his guard down and relax? Spend his time wondering how to make her smile more often instead of digging up information that will likely insure she'll never smile at him again?

"Jars? No, just some labels with a fruit border. I

ordered them from a catalog Dobs has. I figured they'd look nicer than masking tape and . . . What's wrong?"

"Nothing. Sounds great. Just surprised you'd take on the added expense. But I guess if you're already paying for a post office box . . ." He purposely let his words trail off.

"I don't have a box. I told Letty to look for a package for Ann Fielding and hold it for me. It's pretty informal around here. And the labels only cost a few dollars. Or should I say jars."

It was exactly the information he'd been fishing for. So why did he want to tell her to shut up and not reveal anything more? Why did he want to tell her to be careful before she told him too much and discovered she'd have to run again—only this time she'd have to hide from him too?

At least he knew she hadn't laid a paper trail for anyone to pin down her exact location. *Yeah, one person stalking her is enough*, his inner voice jeered.

"Here," he reached for the list, "I'll get this and the feed while you're getting your mail."

She looked up and smiled uncertainly, but handed him the wrinkled piece of paper. "Okay, put it on the counter. I'll help with what's left when I get back."

Kane watched her leave, then turned to look for the feed. He let his shoulders slump a little. This was turning into a headache he didn't need. He'd tackled far more dangerous, complex jobs than this one, but one freckle-faced, redheaded secretary turns a friendly smile his way, and he's tied into a million knots wondering what he should do.

"What you should do is build her a few shelves, hightail it back to Boise, and tell Sam Perkins to stick his money and hire some other idiot to track down his wife," he muttered under his breath as he heaved a fifty-pound sack of sweet feed over his shoulder. He winced at the pain in his palm, knowing he'd opened the cut again but not caring. The mere thought of some other man stalking her and dragging her back to that hair-sprayed, cap-toothed shark of a bank president . . .

Who happened to be her husband. "Dammit."

"Problem, son?" Dobs asked.

Kane heaved the feed onto the floor in front of the counter. "No. Mind if I leave this here while I pick up a few things?"

"Suit yourself."

Kane didn't miss the look Dobs sent out the open doorway toward the post office. He knew the man was dying for the least provocation to discuss Annie again. So why wasn't he rushing to give him one? Kane put the question and the store owner out of his mind and moved over to a shelf loaded with a variety of canned goods.

"Didn't want to say nuthin' with the girl standing right outside the door," Dobs began, as if they'd been talking for some time.

Kane let out a small sigh. So Dobs had known she was there too. He grabbed a couple of cans of soup and moved over to the boxed goods. "About what?" he asked.

Dobs skirted the counter and stopped where he could carry on a quiet conversation, but still keep his eye on the door.

"Now don't take this the wrong way or nuthin'," he said, his gruff voice lowered. "But I'm wantin' to know what your business is with Ann . . . er, Miz Fielding."

Kane paused slightly in his shopping, but was careful to keep a placid expression on his face. "I believe you were the one who pointed out she needed help."

"So that's all there is to it?"

Kane wanted to ask the little tyrant who the hell he thought he was, Annie's guardian? But he knew better. He also knew Dobs was leading up to something, and it wasn't Kane's work qualifications.

"Yeah, I'm building shelves and repairing the barn in exchange for using the bunkhouse for a while."

Dobs shifted closer. "Don't con an old con man, son. I seen the way you look at her."

Kane tensed, his grip on the box of cereal, threatening to send bran flakes flying all over the store.

"Now don't get riled. I'm thinking a man like you might be what she needs. Her being on the run and all."

Kane gave up all pretense of disinterest. In the

blink of an eye, he shelved the groceries he'd been carrying and pulled the little shop owner halfway down the aisle. Pushing his face even with Dobs, he said, "What makes you think she's running from something?"

Dobs didn't even blink at the rough treatment. In fact, his eyes twinkled as if he'd gotten the exact response from Kane he'd wanted. "I've been around these mountains a long time. Survived floods, blizzards, droughts." The twinkle died. "And I know the difference between predator and prey. She's got prey written all over her pretty face. She's not here for no rest. Damn girl's killing herself to make a go of it. Now me, I just want to make sure she's got a fightin' chance." His small gray eyes narrowed. "You gonna be the one to give it to her?"

Kane's grip relaxed. It had been a long time since he'd been maneuvered quite so effectively. He thought of his grandmother and wasted a second wondering who'd have won in a matchup, she or Dobs.

He had no desire to answer the man. He even turned toward the shelves with the idea of continuing his shopping as if their little discussion hadn't happened.

So it came as a surprise to him when he looked the man square in the eye and said, "Yeah. No one will touch her while I'm here." *Including me*, he added silently.

Dobs grinned, revealing a gold tooth and more

than a few empty spaces. "Good. Wouldn't want you hunting the wrong quarry."

Before Kane could react to the remark, Dobs ambled back behind the counter and disappeared again.

FIVE

Elizabeth came out of the post office in time to see Kane stow a box of what looked like groceries in the back of the pickup. There was another one the same size already there, along with two bales of hay and a bag of feed up by the cab. She hurried across the gravel road.

"I'm sorry. I guess I got carried away talking to Letty. You didn't have to do that."

"She's the postmistress, right?" Kane shut the tailgate with a loud clang.

"Postmistress, phone operator, and local busybody." She smiled dryly. "I made the mistake of asking about her grandson, who she'd told me on my last visit had gotten the measles, and that was all it took."

"Guess she doesn't have many people to talk to."

Elizabeth's smile turned a bit wicked, and she

leaned a little closer to Kane. "I think she's got something going with Dobs," she whispered.

She was rewarded with one of Kane's half-smiles. It did such stunning things to his smooth, strong features that it took her a moment to recover. Only when Kane moved toward the driver's side of the truck did she snap out of it and hurry after him.

"I'll drive," he announced as he opened the door and swept a hand in front of him. When she started to protest, he said, "Hop in or I put you in."

Her eyes widened a bit at the command, but she quickly followed his orders. Considering the way his smile had affected her, the thought of him putting those large hands anywhere on her body . . . Not a good idea.

They'd been bouncing over the rutted mountain road for a few minutes when the silence finally got to her. "I made a few calls from the post office." He didn't so much as blink, but she sensed he knew who she'd been calling. "I only got through to two names. Mr. Williams and Mr. Donegan." She'd also tried her brother's apartment. No answer. Again.

"And?"

She knew from the way he sat there that he wasn't concerned with what she might have found out. She was almost tempted to lie, just to see if it would get a reaction out of him, but she couldn't. Both men had praised Kane as if he were their personal patron saint. And to her eternal frustration, they'd both also managed to effectively endorse the man while not revealing one additional whit of personal information.

"And you're still hired," she grumbled, ignoring the slight twitch of his lips, knowing he'd read her hesitation correctly.

She shifted to glance out the rear window and remembered the groceries. She reached for her canvas tote that sat on the bench seat between them. "I completely forgot about the food. Here, let me pay—"

"No need."

"But I didn't mean for you to—"

"I know. Like I said, don't worry about it."

She knew there was more in those boxes than she'd had on the list. "At least let me pay for—"

"I said let it go."

"My half," she finished stubbornly. "I was only trying to help. I didn't think you had . . ." This time she let her words trail off as it occurred to her that what she'd been about to say probably would have offended him.

"Money?" he finished.

She winced. "It's nothing to be ashamed of. After all, it isn't as if I don't understand." She tried for a tone of self-deprecating humor to take the sting out of the conversation, but his jawline remained rock-hard.

"What made you think I didn't have any money?" he said.

She turned to look at him. "I don't know, I

guess I assumed that finances were tight, since you were looking to trade labor for board."

"If you recall, I made the offer because of your situation, not mine."

"But you said yourself you're a wanderer, that you move from place to place. So it wasn't exactly unreasonable of me to think you weren't rolling in it."

"Apology accepted."

She sputtered and turned to tell him she hadn't said anything to apologize for, only to see the corner of his mouth curving slightly. She chuckled softly at having been played so smoothly.

The soft sound brought his head around. The moment their eyes met, her smile faded. After another second, so did his. Tension filled the small cab until a jolt of the truck as it hit a rut brought Kane's attention back to the road. Elizabeth turned to gaze out of her window, half expecting to find it steamed over.

They rode in silence for several minutes before she gave in to her curiosity. "Are you really happy moving around the way you do? Do you ever dream of doing something else?"

He was silent for so long, it surprised her when he answered. "I've never thought of it in terms of happiness or sadness. It's simply the way I live."

She shifted sideways so she could look at him while they talked. "Yeah, but don't you ever see yourself doing something else? I mean, what about when you get old? Don't you want a family?"

Out of the corner of her eye, she saw his fingers tighten on the wheel.

"I'm not exactly family-man material."

The pain that knifed through Elizabeth at his solemn statement was surprisingly sharp. She didn't want to hurt him, but maybe the fact that he'd answered at all meant he wanted to talk about it but didn't know how.

"That's not what I asked," she said gently. When he didn't respond, she switched tactics, not analyzing why it was suddenly so important to her to draw him out. "You named your horse Sky Dancer. I remember you saying your grandmother's name was Cloud Dancer. Any connection?"

"Yes, there's a connection."

"She's beautiful. I watched you work her yesterday." She realized what she'd admitted to, but brazened it out when he didn't comment. "Do you ride everywhere you go?"

"No. I drive a truck most of the time. I have a few friends who take care of my horses."

"You have more than one?"

He shot her a wry grin. "Yes, I have more than one."

She opened her mouth to ask another question, but he cut her off.

"Did anyone ever tell you that there's such a thing as being too curious?"

She wanted to smile at his gentle sarcasm, but memories of Sam and the volatile accusations he'd flung at her that night in his car outside of Joe

Twyler's house flashed through her brain, stealing away any chance she had of taking Kane's words lightly. "Once or twice." She'd been aiming for the same dry sarcasm, but it didn't quite come out that way.

Kane slowed the truck after the next curve and used the upcoming flat stretch as an excuse to look at her. She'd turned her attention out her side window. He couldn't see her face, but her shoulders had slumped slightly. And even more telling, the vitality and energy that typically emanated from her had vanished.

He looked back to the road, reining in the urge to swear. Why had he let her probe him so deeply? Worse yet, why had he answered her? He'd ruthlessly interrogated dozens of people without feeling a twinge of conscience as long as it got the job done. And he'd never once had the slightest urge to divulge personal information.

But the fact remained that he had told her things he didn't discuss with anyone. And the part of him that had spent over a decade dissecting every nuance of a person's reaction, looking for the fastest way to extract information, knew that giving her a piece of himself practically ensured that she'd answer anything he asked. But if he wanted to take advantage, he had to do it now, while she was feeling vulnerable.

So do it. Go on. Ask her. What are you waiting for?

His stomach burned as he swallowed the bile

that lurched upward. He was going to do it. Exploit her interest in him, abuse her trust. He really was a bastard. But then, he'd never kidded himself about that.

"Annie, are you up here because you discovered something about . . . someone?" He paused, grinding his teeth, but it was too late to stop now. "A lover or maybe a . . . a husband? Something this person wouldn't want known?"

She'd given every indication of being a person who'd been dealt some harsh realities. He was positive it concerned Sam, and he'd begun to wonder if she'd discovered he was being unfaithful. It would certainly explain the cock-and-bull story Sam had handed him. Someone in his social position wouldn't want news like that to get out.

He was so convinced he was right, he steeled himself for the inevitable flood of tears and choked recantation of every horrible detail.

Which was why he almost drove the truck off the side of the road when she gaped at him, then flung her head back and began laughing.

Completely thrown, he had no idea how to respond. Not that she would have heard anything. She was laughing so hard at this point, she'd wrapped her arms around her middle.

He hated feeling so helpless, but even more, he hated being made to feel like a fool. So he clamped his jaw shut and set about getting them both home in one piece. The sooner the better.

"I'm . . . I'm sorry," she gasped. "It's

just . . ." She paused to stifle another chuckle with her hand. "Has anyone told *you* that you're the master of understatement?"

After a few minutes, her laughter died down to an occasional giggle.

He forced himself to keep his attention on the road, afraid if he so much as glanced her way, he'd set her off again. And men thought women's tears were tough to handle. He still didn't know what to make of her outburst.

The rickety Lazy F sign appeared as he rounded the last curve. He'd just passed under it when another muffled sound penetrated his thoughts. Thinking she was holding in renewed laughter, he lost his patience and turned to face her.

Only to discover she hadn't been smothering laughter at all. Her head was bent, and small shiny tracks glistened on her cheeks. In that second, a tremor rocked her slender frame as she held in a sob.

"Aw hell." Kane let the truck drift to a stop, but suddenly didn't know what his next move should be. He lifted his hand, intending to reach for her, to take her in his arms, offer her some comfort and an apology for setting off her crying jag in the first place. But he didn't. He let his hand drop to the seat between them. Maybe he'd been wrong about tears being easier.

"Annie?" He tried to keep his voice gentle, but the word sounded almost hoarse to his ears.

She stilled for a second, as if she'd just realized

that they'd stopped moving. Then she subtly shifted away, toward her side window.

"Annie, I'm sorry."

"It's okay," she said, her voice rough with the effort of holding in the tears. "You couldn't have realized . . ." She didn't finish. Another slight tremor shook her frame. "Could we go home, please?" she whispered.

Kane felt like something that lived under a rock. Had she really loved Perkins so much? The more time he spent with her, the harder he found it to picture Annie and Sam as a loving couple.

Or maybe it was because he wanted so badly for them not to be.

"Yeah, I'll take you home," he said softly. He checked the urge to slam his foot on the gas pedal. The sun was barely a laserlike ray over the horizon as he pulled in front of the small ranch house. He'd been a fool to let his emotions get involved. Sam wanted his wife back, and it was obvious she was dying inside over whatever had happened. So he'd reunite the lovesick lovebirds, take his money, and ride off into the sunset. Alone. Again.

And it was his own damn fault that he'd wasted even a second wondering if it could end any other way.

"You go on inside. I'll take care of the stuff in the back," he said after he shut the engine off.

She took a deep breath, wiped her face on the sleeve of her T-shirt, and slowly turned to face him.

The waning light cast her tear-streaked face in soft shadows.

"I don't know what came over me. Nerves, I guess. But you didn't deserve such an hysterical response to your question. I'm sorry, it's just that . . ." She ducked her head for a moment, then looked back up at him. "I really thought that I'd begun to come to terms with it. The stress and all." She chuckled, but it was a harsh sound that made Kane wince. "Obviously I haven't even scratched the surface."

"The offer I made still stands."

She lifted her eyebrows in question.

"To listen. I may not be much on conversation, but I make a great listener."

She seemed to study him for a moment. "Oh, I don't know, Eyes of the Hawk," she said softly. "I imagine you're pretty good at whatever you choose to do."

"Yeah, well, sometimes the choices you make don't count for a hill of beans. Sometimes they're already made for you." Feeling distinctly uncomfortable with the turn of the conversation and more than a little aroused by visions of one particular skill he'd like to prove to her he *was* pretty good at, he opted to bail out before he embarrassed either of them any further. "If you need me, you know where I am." He opened the door and jumped down.

When the sun finally dropped over the horizon, it got dark very fast. So Elizabeth wasn't certain if she'd seen correctly, but she could have sworn

Kane's complexion was a shade or two darker when he'd hopped down from the truck.

Funny. She'd come to think that he could be angered or insulted, even amused by her comments. But never embarrassed. It was an intriguing thought.

She'd been so caught up in her own maelstrom of emotions, she hadn't paid much attention to how Kane had taken her unusual outburst. But speculating on his reaction was a welcome reprieve from analyzing her recent hysteria.

With a renewed sense of energy, she met him at the tail gate. "I'll take the food in, if you want to take the truck around to the barn and unload the hay."

The tail gate creaked as he lowered it. He didn't say anything, just pulled the two boxes forward, pushing the lighter one toward her and grabbing the other.

She didn't force the issue, but lugged her box toward the front door. She felt him moving behind her, the old wood boards on the porch groaning in protest under his booted heels. He propped the box on his hip and reached over her shoulder to grab the screen.

The sight of his strong, rough hand gripping the frame heightened her awareness of his nearness and she fumbled with the door handle. Once inside, she moved quickly through the small living room to the kitchen. Even in the dark, she knew the layout. She

put the box down on the counter and went to turn
on the propane lamp that sat on the table.

Kane came into the room as she turned to find
the lamp. Her searching fingers hit denim. Warm,
hard denim. She snatched her hand away. Jeez, what
was with her tonight? First the sight of his long,
strong fingers made her want to drop her box and
fall into arms she knew would be just as powerful.
Then the mere brush of her hand against his clothes
made her wonder if he had similar thoughts.

"Um, here let me feel the table and make sure
there's enough room," she said quickly. She could
have sworn she heard him groan softly. She knew
the box wasn't that heavy. In the next second her
hands brushed on the bottle of alcohol and cotton
balls she'd brought down earlier to tend to his splinter.

She caught the bottle before it tilted over and
quickly moved the stuff aside. She reached out carefully and grabbed the front two corners of the box,
guiding it to the table.

Once it was down, she said, "Give me a second
to find the lantern." Where had she left it?

"Annie."

She froze. His voice was deeper than normal.
The way he'd said her name . . . as if . . . She
stopped her thoughts right there.

"Annie," he repeated, only this time with a sense
of urgency that made her automatically turn toward
the sound.

"What?" She stood very still, part of her wanting to squint and force her night vision to adjust more quickly, the rest of her wanting to stay secure in the anonymity the darkness provided.

Large hands suddenly gripped her shoulders. Startled, she reached out to steady herself, grasping his forearms. She looked up to where she knew his eyes would be and found them. She shivered. And she wasn't the least bit cold.

"Do you love him?" His voice was dark and steamy, like the air surrounding them.

"Do I—What?" she said with a gasp, completely unprepared for the question.

She heard him heave a sigh of . . . disgust? Was it with her? Or himself? And why? She didn't know which question to ask first, or whether to tell him it wasn't any of his damn business. She also knew the scene in the truck deserved at least a little explanation. But what could she tell him without jeopardizing her safety—or his? His next question saved her from figuring it out.

"Do you want to go back to him?"

The very idea made her throat close convulsively over the sudden heave of her stomach muscles. She tried to answer him but couldn't seem to get the words out.

"Never mind. It's none of my business."

She felt his hands shift on her shoulders and tightened her grip on his forearms, suddenly not wanting him to break the contact. She lifted a hand to his cheek, but her fingers barely brushed over the light stubble on his jaw before he pulled his head away. She quickly grabbed his forearm again. "Kane, don't—"

"I need to tend to Sky Dancer. If you want to leave this, I'll help you in the morning."

She could feel the tension in the tightly coiled muscles clenched beneath her fingertips. She wanted to lift his hands from her shoulders and cradle them against her face. She wanted him to fold her against his chest, to lower his mouth to hers.

She slid her hands toward his wrists, but in the next instant he broke contact and stepped away.

"Kane, I can put away groceries later, just don't—" She broke off as she heard the front screen slap shut. "Leave yet," she finished softly.

The tears she'd shed in the truck had been her first in three months. She'd felt as if she'd shed at least enough for a year. The hot sting behind her closed eyelids proved otherwise. She groped for a chair and sank into it, feeling as if her last remaining energy had left with Kane.

She'd never felt so confused in all her life. Other than what had happened the night she'd followed Sam, the last few hours qualified as the most draining she'd experienced.

Kane had blown into her life like a lone hawk riding the summer wind. He'd appeared at a time when her confidence in her instincts was at an all-time low. Was she lonely and drawn to him because he happened to be the only one for miles around with a sympathetic ear?

There was Dobs, and Letty, of course, but she

had to admit she'd certainly never felt like unloading on them. They didn't look like Kane. Maybe that was it. Even in her mentally exhausted state, it didn't take a genius to realize that the man was both gorgeous and enigmatic. It was only natural that she would respond to him.

The overwhelming need she'd felt to have him pull her into his arms and hold her against his nice broad chest . . . that was her hormones talking.

She folded her arms on the table and rested her forehead on top of them. She was full of horse manure.

Deep down, below the confusion and dread, the stress and anxiety of being forced to hide, she knew she'd have responded to Kane no matter what the circumstances. He was vital and strong, with that tantalizing hint of mystery. And he had integrity by the bushel.

And she had no right to let him become more involved in her life.

The tears began to flow again. This time she let them go, no longer bothering to hold back the sobs.

"Annie?"

She hadn't heard him come in. He laid his hands on her shoulders at the same time he said her name. She choked simultaneously on a sob and a scream, unable to fight him as he lifted her to her feet.

"Come here," he said gruffly.

His arms tightened around her, pulling her smaller, softer body tightly against his larger, harder one. He lifted one hand to her nape and tucked her head gently to his chest. It was broad and warm and made her feel so secure. She realized then that she didn't want to fight him. Not when she was finally getting what she'd wanted all along.

"Kane," she said, the sound muffled against the soft cotton of his shirt.

"Shhh. Stop trying to carry the whole world on your shoulders. Let someone hold you. Let me."

His gentle urging was her undoing. It came too soon on the heels of her decision to stay away from him, too soon for her to recoup the strength she'd depleted with her crying jag. So she let herself go and curled into his strength, drawing energy from his warmth and the steady beat of his heart.

Just for a few minutes. Only a few minutes.

Kane bit his cheek to stifle the groan that rose in his throat. The feel of her, soft and trembling in his arms, was almost more than he could bear. His body had hardened the second she'd relaxed against him. He fought to keep his hands gentle when all he wanted to do was tighten them on her hips and drag her closer. He didn't even allow himself to rest his chin on her hair, afraid if he smelled the sweet scent that seemed always to linger on her, he'd have to bury his face in the wild red curls and savor it.

She needs comforting not seducing, he reminded himself. She'd needed it before, but he'd wisely turned away and left. When another sob wracked her body, he cursed inwardly. This was all his fault. He shouldn't have pushed her so soon. His body pulsed behind the fly of his jeans as she moved against him.

And he definitely shouldn't have gotten back out of the truck when he'd heard her first choked sob.

"I don't know what I'm going to do, Kane," she said, her voice thick with emotion.

"Can you . . . do you think you can work it out?" Kane asked through gritted teeth. Lord, he wished he were anywhere but there. With her. Holding her. Yet, when she burrowed even more deeply into his arms, he knew he didn't want to be anywhere else.

"No."

Her response was adamant and immediate. And Kane felt something close to shame for the surge of pleasure he got from her succinct answer. "Is it the money?"

She let her cheek rest on his chest as she answered. "Money? What do you mean?"

Kane wasn't sure how to phrase the next question. "I mean, it looks as if he cut you off, or you wouldn't be picking berries in the middle of nowhere to survive."

She was silent for a moment. He felt her tense, fighting another halting shudder as she drew in a breath.

"It's one of the results, but not the reason. Why?"

The need to protect her had been strong from the moment he'd laid eyes on her. Now that he had her in his arms, he couldn't deny that those same instincts were urging him to help her. Despite what he was beginning to feel, what he suspected he could share with a woman like her, if all she'd accept from him was money, than that was what he'd offer.

"Do you . . . did you want a lawyer or something? I mean, is there a reason you had to go so far away? To get away from him? A . . . physical reason?"

She stiffened and yanked herself from his arms. "I . . . I can't tell you anything more, Kane. I'm sorry. I wish I could . . ." She pulled in an audible breath. "Maybe you'd better go."

"Go?"

"Yes. Well, no. I mean—" She sniffled, then sighed heavily. "Thank you for offering support. I'd be lying if I said it didn't feel great to lean on someone. It's just . . . this is more complicated than it sounds, and I . . . I don't want to talk about it anymore. I can't. Do you understand?"

"What I understand is that you're running yourself ragged up here, trying to survive," he said, not giving a damn that his voice was harsh. She had him so tied up in knots, it was a wonder he could speak at all. "You obviously don't think going back is the answer. Fine. But you won't last the winter up here, Annie. So you're going to have to deal with it pretty damn soon. And I don't exactly see a long line of people standing around wanting to help."

"I know," she said softly.

There was so much defeat in those two words

that a great deal of his anger fled. He took a step toward her but didn't touch her. "So let me."

"It isn't that simple. I can't let you get involved in this. You don't know what you'd be getting into."

"Then tell me so I do know." His patience was close to snapping. He was going purely on instinct now, and it was wreaking havoc with his self-control. "I want to help you, Annie. But you have to tell me everything." He wanted to reach out and pull her to him again, but he held his ground.

"Why? Why do you want to stick your neck out for me?"

It was a damn good question. Only he didn't think she wanted to hear his instinctive response. She'd made an unexpected impact on him, and in only a few short days. He wasn't too comfortable with the knowledge of his growing feelings for her and certainly wasn't ready to share them. So he gave her a truth they could both handle.

"Because I know something is wrong here. And I know I can help. I can't walk away from that. Is that so hard to understand?"

"Your sense of integrity is rare, no matter what you believe," she said quietly. "But what makes you think you can help me? You don't even know what I'm running from."

There. He'd gotten her to trust him enough to admit it. But the feeling of triumph was overshadowed by the knowledge that she must have run for a damn good reason. "Then tell me," he urged quietly. This time he did give in to the need to touch her. His eyes had long ago adapted to the dark, and he unerringly reached for her hips. He tugged her a step closer to him, struggling to keep his hold light.

She tensed. He could feel her muscles coil under his fingertips and sensed she was a breath away from running. He couldn't let her do that. Not now when he was so close. He had to get her to tell him everything.

He had a split-second urge to pull her the rest of the way into his arms and kiss her until she was too dizzy to deny him anything. But the very last thing she needed right now was him coming on to her. It was amazing she'd let him offer what comfort he had without delivering a stinging slap to his cheek. He swallowed hard on the knowledge that maybe he'd feel better if she had. It might have gone a long way to assuaging his guilt over knowing he'd wanted to offer her a whole lot more than a friendly shoulder.

His first priority, however, was to get her to talk. Which left one other alternative. He knew it would be a lot easier for her to risk part of herself if he made the same commitment.

"Annie, there are things about me you don't know." He heard a strangled sound. Had she actually laughed? He didn't pause to pursue it, knowing he wouldn't have the nerve to do this twice. "I've spent a lot of years . . . studying human behavior. I've done some favors, worked for some people who have a lot of contacts. Powerful ones." He gave in to the need to tug her another inch closer. "Let me help you," he whispered.

He could see the glistening sheen of her eyes as she stared back at him. He felt her soften beneath his fingers and had to swallow the urge to shout in triumph.

"I really shouldn't . . ." She angled her body away from him, then blew out a long breath. "I want to, Kane. But this is so hard."

"I know it is. And I can't force you to trust me." He tugged her back around and unconsciously lifted his hand to her face. The absence of light heightened his sense of touch. Her skin was warm and soft, damp with the tears he'd caused her to shed. Very slowly he lowered his head and placed the softest kiss he could manage on each silver-streaked cheek. Her warm skin and sweet scent burned a path straight to his heart. But when she gasped, his desire to taste the rest of her rocked through him so hard, he almost dropped to his knees.

Using up all the willpower he had left, he let his hands drop to his sides in tightly clenched fists and stepped away.

"Why don't you find the lantern," he said, his voice barely more than a gruff rasp. "We'll talk while we put this stuff away."

SIX

The soft glow of the propane lamp lit the small square room in a muted golden tone, casting into shadows the dinginess that even her extensive cleaning couldn't erase.

Elizabeth kept as much distance between herself and Kane as possible as she stored the groceries and issued directions. But while they'd managed to keep from touching again, she found it impossible not to make occasional eye contact. His black gaze was almost tangible, making her efforts at avoiding physical contact seem silly.

"I'll use this empty box for the few things to be stored in the spring house," she said.

"No icebox?"

"There's a cold-storage bin in the root cellar, but I haven't gotten around to cleaning down there."

"Given the shape of the rest of the house, I imagine it's not the friendliest place in the world."

Elizabeth stilled for a brief moment before continuing to arrange the items in the cardboard box. It was more than a little disconcerting that he never took what she said at face value, that he always understood the deeper meaning. Yet, it was oddly comforting too.

"Yeah, well, I've never been thrilled with cold, musty places. We're talking major Vincent Price material."

"I can check it out for you."

Again, she paused. "I don't think that's necessary, the spring house is plenty big enough and close to the back door." She looked up and found his gaze on her again, as she'd known it would be. "But thanks for the offer."

After they'd found the lamp, he'd let her slip into the familiar routine of stowing the groceries without pushing any further for the explanation she'd promised him. She hadn't expected the reprieve. Between her emotional outburst earlier and the riot of feelings that had exploded inside her the instant she'd felt his lips brush against her cheek, she more than welcomed the chance to regain her bearings.

Judging from the flat, unreadable expression that had returned to his eyes, his offer of help was simply that, not a calculated move to remind her of his earlier offer.

It did anyway. She tamped down the uneasy feeling that maybe she shouldn't be in such a hurry to rely on her instincts again. Especially where Kane Hawthorne was concerned.

Hoping to quell her sudden tangle of nerves, she turned back to packing the box. "However, I reserve the right to call for help if I find another snake in the spring house," she said with a light smile. "Spiders and mice I can handle; anything with legs. But creatures that can move on the ground that fast without any feet, I don't trust."

"The trick is not to let them see you coming."

Elizabeth darted a glance at him. "Yeah, well, you'd know plenty about that," she teased.

She felt her pulse accelerate when she was rewarded with another of his rare smiles. It was no more than a slight upward curve at the corners of his mouth, but it managed to push a button. Lord knew how she'd respond if he ever flashed a real one. She'd probably spontaneously combust.

"What's so funny?"

She realized with a start that she'd been staring at him, and given the thread of her thoughts, she could only wonder what he'd seen on her face. She felt her cheeks warm and hoped the soft lighting kept it her secret. "Nothing really. It's just . . . well, you look so different when you smile. I guess I wondered why you don't do it more often."

His smile didn't disappear, as she'd half expected it to, but from where he stood leaning on the counter a few feet away, she saw his jaw tighten and a tiny muscle twitch at the corner of his eye. Another sore subject? Smiling?

Just as suddenly, the teasing, easy mood they'd shared for the past few minutes vanished. Again she looked for salvation in the newly filled box in front of her. Grabbing the corners, she lifted it, her motions made stiff by the sudden awkwardness she felt. She didn't hear him leave his post by the counter, but as soon as she'd settled the heavy weight in her arms, he relieved her of the burden.

"I didn't mean to make you uncomfortable," he said quietly. "You were just being nice." He stepped back and moved to go around her.

Without conscious thought, Elizabeth blocked his path. "I wasn't 'just being nice,' I was being sincere. You're a handsome man who happens to look pretty sensational when you smile. It's not a crime, you know."

All she got was a noncommittal grunt as he pushed past her and walked to the back door.

She didn't bother hiding her smile. It felt too good. Besides, this time she had no doubt. "Why, Kane Hawthorne," she called after him, "I do believe you're blushing."

The slap of the screen door was his only response. It wasn't until she turned and went about storing the other empty boxes, that it occurred to her he hadn't said whether he was coming back. Even though it was dark, it really wasn't very late. And it wasn't as if either of them had to be up at dawn. Somehow she doubted he was going to let her have the entire night to change her mind about telling him her story.

A frown crossed her face. Why was he so insistent on helping her? Was he really the honorable guy his references claimed he was? What else could he be? she asked silently. If he had some other nefarious scheme in mind, he certainly could have carried it out by now. So that left . . . what?

An honest man with a strong streak of integrity, her mind instantly responded.

"Yeah, and it's no secret how reliable a judge of character you are," she muttered.

She sighed and rested her back against the counter. She immediately noticed there were two bottles of beer sitting on the table. The boxes had hidden them from view before. She hadn't taken them out, so Kane must have.

Well, that answered her earlier question.

She twisted the caps off with the tail of her T-shirt and headed out to the back stoop. They'd likely cave in the front porch if they both sat on it at the same time.

She perched on the wider bottom step and stretched her legs out in front of her while she waited for Kane.

She heard the spring door squeak on its hinges, which meant she had roughly thirty seconds to decide what to say to him. Two things hit her simultaneously as she heard him—or rather felt him—come closer. One: She did trust him, at least enough to use the shoulder he was willing to provide; And two:

Although she had no doubt a man like Kane could have inspired a long list of loyal contacts over his years of wandering, the bottom line was listening to her was all he could do.

Her brother was the only man who could give her the kind of help she needed. Not Kane. Not a man also called Eyes of the Hawk.

"Nickel for your thoughts."

"A whole nickel?"

Kane took the beer Annie offered, but when she looked up at him and the rising moon reflected in her eyes, he elected to lean against the house and leave the step to her.

He shrugged. "Inflation." He forced his gaze from the graceful line of her legs all stretched out and begging to be admired. He had no doubt he could spend a rather enjoyable evening doing just that. But not tonight, maybe never. He needed information. "I figure you got a fortune's worth of thoughts running around inside your head. Consider it a small down payment."

He stifled a sigh as she pulled her legs in. She tucked her feet under the step, looping her arms around her shins and resting her chin on her knees. Bolstering her nerve and girding for battle, he thought, wishing she didn't have demons to fight. Wondering why in the hell it was so important to him to fight them for her.

"Do you have a home anywhere, Kane? I mean, are you always on the road?"

Her question surprised him. Kane grimaced, determined *not* to let her sidetrack him into talking about himself again. Nonetheless, he thought about the small apartment he presently rented. No, it wasn't any more of a home to him than the P.O. box he kept in Pocatello. "Not really."

He'd thought himself long past the point of being bothered by that simple truth. He had no home, nothing he could claim as his own, except a truck and a few horses. He'd never found anything else worth claiming. So why did admitting as much to her hurt? He gazed down at her. And why did it feel like a lie?

"I think I know what that's like. At least, a little."

Her soft voice jerked him back to the present. He realized then that he'd reached a decision, had probably made it the day he'd met her. As of this moment, he was no longer working for Sam Perkins. He couldn't tell her that, of course. Not if he had any hopes of helping her.

And he would help her. It was the only thing he had to offer her. When the time came to leave her, he would at least have that to take with him.

"You aren't planning to stay here for the winter." He hadn't phrased it as a question, but she answered anyway.

"I don't want to," she responded carefully.

"If it's not money problems keeping you here, then what? You don't have to go back to him. You said you had a brother, won't he help you?"

"He will if he can."

Her whispered answer barely reached his ears. Louder, she said, "It's more complicated . . . I mean, I just can't go back right now."

Kane crouched down next to her raised knees. Setting the bottle on the ground, he balanced one hand on his thigh and let the other one drop gently on her shoulder. He pressed his fingers lightly, urging her to look at him.

After what seemed like ages, she did. He'd expected the sorrow and uncertainty he found in her soft brown eyes. But what curled his free hand into a tight fist against his thigh was the unmistakable trace of fear he saw as well.

"Did he hurt you, Annie? Did you come all the way out here because you're afraid of him? Of what he might do?"

Even the late hour couldn't cast a shadow dark enough to mask the flash of pure terror in her eyes before she looked away.

He tightened his hold on her shoulder, using what was left of his restraint to keep from yanking her to her feet and doing whatever he felt necessary to get the whole story from her. "Annie," he demanded softly. When she didn't respond, he pulled her until she sat sideways on the steps, her tightly pressed knees tucked between his thighs. She kept her gaze cast downward. "You can't stay here alone."

"I'm not alone," she whispered. Then, even softer, she added, "You're here."

His fingers trembled. "Look at me, Annie. Look at me."

Slowly, she raised her eyes to him, and he could see what she'd been trying to hide. The moon high-lighted their glassy surface, but her cheeks were dry.

"Did he hurt you? I know it's hard, but you have to tell me if I'm going to help you."

His fingertips registered the gentle tremors that raced through her. He ached to pull her into his arms. He wanted to hold her, heal her. He also wanted to kiss her, to taste her again and again, to make love to her. And that was absolutely the last thing she needed from him.

Her gaze locked on his, and his chest tightened.

"I wish you could help me, Hawk. You can't know how much."

"Hawk?" he echoed automatically.

A shaky smile curved her lips. "I don't know where that came from. Your Indian name, I guess. It . . . it suits you."

He fought his immediate physical response, telling himself it was only a nickname.

"Call me whatever you want," he said, trying to sound as if it didn't matter. "But I can't do anything until you tell me why you ran." He refused to let her back away from the truth.

She broke eye contact again and stared downward as she twisted her fingers together. So much tension in such a slender frame.

"Aw hell," he muttered. Giving in to his need to ease her silent torment, he slid onto the step above her and gently turned her so she sat between his thighs with her back to him. He'd expected a fight and didn't quite know what to make of her acquiescence. Not one to dwell on infrequent favors, small or otherwise, he began gently kneading the soft curves at the base of her neck.

She didn't make a single noise, but after several minutes, she did let her head fall slightly forward.

Kane stifled a groan as the moon lit the fine ridge of her spine that peeked out from the top of her loose collar. Acting on instinct, he pressed his thumbs to the center of her back and ran them slowly downward. It was as if he'd unzipped her. Her body sagged, then shivered as he retraced the motion upward. He followed the same motion again, this time wringing a sigh from her as his hands stopped to rest on her shoulders. He forced his fingers to lay gently and not to pull her backward—against his hard, fully aroused, body.

Instead he let his hands drop, his arms resting on his thighs, his chin just above her head. The scent of her hair, the scent of *her*, kept him aroused, but he used the discomfort to remind him of his offer to help.

"Why did you run?" he asked, his voice a rough whisper.

After a long moment in which he felt her shudder as surely as if he were still touching her, she answered.

"Because if he finds me, he'll kill me."

She said it with total conviction. That fact, combined with the undiluted terror he'd witnessed briefly in her eyes, told him she was not exaggerating. Rage filled him. His palms fairly itched with the need to pound something. Preferably flesh. Specifically Sam Perkins's flesh.

He fisted his hands, as much to stem the urge for violence as to prevent him from yanking her into his arms and keeping her there. Paying dearly for his even tone, he asked, "Why here? Doesn't he know about this place?"

"No," she said, her voice still shaky. "I told you before, I'd only been here once. And that was over two decades ago."

"Is the deed in your name? Can he trace you here?" Kane already knew the answers to those questions, but he had to ask. When she was thinking more clearly, she'd surely wonder why he hadn't. He grimaced, hating the duplicity. Telling himself she'd know everything at some point didn't make him feel one whit better.

"The deed is in Matthew's name," she answered, mercifully pulling him from his thoughts. "It's not listed on any of my asset sheets, such as they are. I'm not sure if Matt claims it, but it's probably on his tax statements. I don't think Sam would think to track them down. I didn't even remember it until I saw the picture in Matt's apartment."

Kane winced, glad she was facing away from him. "Sam. Tell me about him, Annie. What would make him want to kill you? Is it because you finally stood up to him and escaped?"

"It's not like that. I mean, until . . . he never hurt me, not physically, if that's what you're thinking."

"Tell me what I'm supposed to think, Annie."

"I . . . uh . . ." She gulped, the sound audible. "You were right. I know something about him he doesn't want revealed. It could . . . destroy his reputation. His whole life."

Damn. He'd figured as much. A mistress. He ached for the anguish she must be going through. As if the terror of being hunted wasn't enough, she was dealing with rejection as well. The latter, an emotion he was on intimate terms with.

And all the money in the world wouldn't have stopped Kane from killing Sam Perkins with his bare hands if he had appeared at that moment.

"Must be one hell of an affair if he's willing to kill to keep it a secret." He wanted to kick himself when she flinched. "I'm sorry, that was a lousy thing to say."

"Don't apologize. I only wish that were the case." She laughed, and the flat sound chilled him. "The night I followed him, that's what I suspected." She tipped her head back, her gaze directed at the star-filled sky. "What a fool I was to think that I would have been devastated by that truth." Another bark of laughter. "Now I'd gladly line the women up if that was all he wanted."

Kane's mind whirred with this new information. He'd jumped way off base, and it took a moment to reconfigure the facts. If it wasn't a sex scandal Perkins was afraid of, that left one other alternative.

"Are you saying he's involved in something illegal?"

She shook her head. "You know, when I finally figured out what he was doing, I was so stunned, the legal implications didn't cross my mind."

Kane had only to tilt his head to the side to see the slight quiver of her chin. It was the only indication that she was holding on to her anger with a grip that was tenuous at best.

"Something else happened to change that." It was a statement meant to encourage not question her story.

She nodded, the motion small and tight. "Oh yeah."

"What was he doing, Annie? The night you followed him, where did he go?"

"He was attending a . . . meeting. In Hunnicutt. At Joe Twyler's house."

Kane knew of the small town. It was a dozen or so miles outside of Boise. The man's name was familiar also, but the connection didn't come through. She took care of that with her next statement.

"Aside from Sam and Hunnicutt's mayor, the chief of the local police department and several influential Boise businessmen were there. There were others, but I didn't recognize them. Not that it mattered."

Kane let out a long, slow breath. Damn, damn, damn. Annie hadn't been lying about the trouble she was in. As a matter of fact, to his knowledge, she'd never lied to him about anything. An honest woman. He grimaced. Just what Sam Perkins didn't need.

"How did you know these people? Do they know you? Do they know you saw them?"

She waved her hand as if to slow him down, then slumped forward to rest her chin on her knees, raking her fingers through her tangled hair. Her fingers shook, and she eventually dropped her hand to clasp her other one around her shins.

Kane felt as if he'd kicked a defenseless kitten. He took another deep breath, struggling to keep a hold on his control. A thousand questions lay right on the tip of his tongue. But what Annie didn't need was him grilling her, making her feel like the criminal instead of the victim.

"I'm sorry. You're throwing a lot at me." He fought a surprising smile when her posture once again became rigid and defensive. Maybe there was more tigress in his kitten than he'd credited her with. "I know I asked you to. Just give me a second to think this through."

"Why? How long does it take to decide to cut and run?"

Kane hadn't missed the plea underlying her tough-as-nails demand. "Annie—"

"I wouldn't blame you if you did, you know." Her spine slackened some, her voice when she spoke was more rough than harsh. "I knew from the start it would be like asking for the moon."

Before he could think to do otherwise, Kane followed his instincts and tugged her backward, cradling her against him. At the last moment, he regained enough control to settle for looping his arms loosely around her shoulders, letting them dangle in front of her chin, while his own rested lightly on the top of her head.

"If you asked for it, I think I'd find myself trying like hell to get it for you."

She flinched at his softly spoken avowal, but it had been said, and he wouldn't let her pull away.

"Why? Why would you do that, or any of this for me? You don't even know me."

"I suspect I know you better than most." She didn't deny it so he pushed on, ignoring the danger signals blaring in his head to quit now before he tore apart everything he'd accomplished. "And I think maybe the same could be said of you."

She was silent for a moment. "Then that's a very sad thing."

"Why?"

"Because I feel as if I don't know you at all, Hawk."

His blood pounded through his body at her softly spoken endearment. And it was an endearment, at least to his mind. To his heart. His body followed his heart and responded accordingly. "Yes, Annie, you do," he said quietly. "More than you think." She stiffened. "You trusted me with your story. Something I don't think you'd have done with another man. True?"

"Maybe that's so, but you can't deny that my judgment isn't the greatest in the world."

Kane swore under his breath. Another thing Perkins had robbed her of, and it was a precious gift. Her self-respect. "Annie, there is no shame in loving someone with all that you are. If that person betrays that love, it is their loss, their shame. For destroying a gift that should have been revered."

Silence followed his terse declaration, forcing him to listen to the echoes of his words in his mind. Thoughts of his grandmother assaulted him. Yes, he knew all about the pain and shame of betraying someone's love. The loss of a precious gift. What was happening to him? Distance, he needed to put Annie at a distance before he made a bigger fool of himself.

No matter what had happened with Perkins, she was bound to him by law. Not to mention vows of love that she obviously took very seriously. Vows that had been wasted on a bastard not worthy of her loyalty. He struggled to pull his control together, to do what he had to do.

Her next words kept him stock-still.

"Did you ever love someone like that, Hawk? Completely? Blindly, maybe?"

His heart fisted in his chest. Her question resurrected another ghost, this pain old and well worn like a talisman rubbed again and again until the sharp edges were too dulled to cut. "Yes. But I didn't have any choice."

"Is this part of what you meant earlier? About not always having the right to choose?"

"It was my mother."

He felt the air leave her body in a long whoosh and fought against turning her in his arms and kissing her, of not stopping until all their hurt disappeared.

"That's one thing I had. I didn't take it for granted, either." She shifted a bit, resting her chin on his forearm but not looking back at him. "That stinks, Kane. I'm sorry."

"Don't be," he started to say, but her hand on his arm stopped the automatic denial.

"For her, Hawk. For her. She's missing one hell of a son."

Kane's throat tightened at the unexpected gift. He blinked hard several times, then gave in and buried his face in her hair. What had he done to deserve finding such truth in a person, only to be put in a position of having to betray it? He wanted to stand and howl at the moon, stomp and yell and argue with the Fates until he got the answers he wanted.

But he didn't. He sat right where he was and let her sweet scent seep into his pores, into his mind, into his heart. Storing up the heady sensations for the day when she would no longer be within his grasp. "Thank you," he said roughly.

She didn't respond except to squeeze his arm gently then turn to face away from him once again. When he could finally manage it, he pulled away from her, leaning his elbows on the step behind him. It took a considerable amount of discipline, all that he had in fact, but he ruthlessly steered his mind back to her revelation, to his original purpose —helping her.

"What did you discover that night? What was Sam doing that was so terrible that he threatened you?"

"It wasn't a threat. I tried to talk to him about it, make him see reason. That didn't work. He poured on the charm, trying to convince me to do what he wanted. He's real good at that. But I . . . couldn't. Not until he explained."

"Did he?"

She shuddered. "No. He got nasty. Violent. I'd . . . I'd never seen him like that." She pulled in a visible breath. "I left him after that night. Checked into a motel until I could figure out what to do next."

"And?"

"And two days later, I was almost run off the road by an old pickup truck with no tags."

Kane had sensed it coming. But he wasn't prepared for the ferocity of his response. "Are you sure he was behind it?" he asked through gritted teeth. "Was he driving?"

"I couldn't see, but I doubt it was Sam. And at first, I really wanted to believe it was a coincidence. A driver with too many beers under his belt. It was a Friday night, and . . . But it wasn't a drunk driver."

"Another attempt?"

She nodded. He gently massaged her shoulders. "I know it's hard. Take your time." Time. Hers was running out, and it was all Kane could do to keep from tearing out of there and back to Boise where he could get his hands on Perkins's scrawny, lily-livered neck. But without all the facts, charging off half-cocked was only likely to get them both hurt.

"What happened?" he urged, as much for his sake as hers. "Another car incident like the first one?"

"Same truck. But this time it was in the underground parking garage in the building I work in. It . . . it was late, and I was the only one around. The headlights . . ." She shuddered. "They blinded me. At the last minute I jumped onto the hood of the car—"

"Son of a good-for-nothing bitch!" Kane roared, unable to control his rage a moment longer. Uncaring how she interpreted his comment or his actions, he pulled her roughly into his lap, this time folding his arms tightly around her and pressing his face against her neck.

"I wanted to go to the police," she murmured against his shirt. "But I got paranoid. I couldn't be sure who was in on it . . ."

His lips found the pulse at her temple. "We'll get him, Annie. I promise you."

She tugged at his arms with her hands, squirming inside his tight embrace. With great reluctance he released her, wanting to apologize for his actions, but unable to lie to her at this point.

To his surprise she huddled closer to him. It took less than a second before his arms closed around her again. It was clear she needed a shoulder, to feel protected.

His heart pounded so loudly under the sweet pressure of her cheek against his chest, it took him a moment to realize she was speaking.

"What?"

"Thank you," she repeated softly. "For this." She looked up at him.

His heart swelled then tightened painfully at the look of admiration he found shining in her eyes. He wanted to tell her how undeserving he was, but she didn't let him.

"Your faith in me is more than I could hope for," she said, ironically echoing his own thoughts. "But I can't let you interfere."

"Why the hell not?" No way was he letting her push him away now.

"Because you'll get hurt."

Kane studied her closely. "I understand the risk, Annie," he said tersely, silently cursing himself for wishing it had been more than basic concern of one human being for another. "I'm willing to take it. It's my decision, and I take responsibility for it."

"But you don't understand the risk. Not fully anyway."

He realized then that there was something she hadn't told him, something important. He lifted her chin and locked his gaze on hers. "Then tell me and let me be the judge."

"The meeting I went to—" she broke off, her chin quivering.

"Annie?"

"I'm sorry, Hawk." She took a deep breath. The sound was uneven and thready. "He . . . Sam is . . . He's a . . ."

"What? What?"

"This is so hard, especially . . ." She pulled in another lungful of air and blurted it out. "Sam went to Twyler's that night to attend a meeting. A meeting of an organization called The Alliance."

"What the hell is The Alliance?"

She reached up and placed her trembling fingertips on his lips as if in silent apology for what she was about to say. "The Alliance is an organization of white supremacists." A lone tear escaped and tracked slowly down her cheek. "Sam is one of the leaders."

SEVEN

Kane went completely still. His brain was numb for a moment as it absorbed the shock, then exploded into activity. "That can't be," he muttered, as his thoughts boiled down to one irrefutable fact. Perkins had hired a half-breed to find his wife. A man with supremacy beliefs—a leader of them, no less—would hardly be hiring a nonwhite person, no matter the necessity.

He didn't realize he was crushing Annie against his chest until she began to struggle. He loosened his arms automatically.

"Kane," she said softly. When he didn't respond, she laid her hand on his cheek. "Hawk?"

He immediately focused on her, on her eyes, which were huge with worry. *Oh, Annie, what have you gone and done?* "What?" he answered hoarsely.

"It's true. I know I'm not mistaken. I listened to

them talk, to their—" she broke off, visibly shoring up another deep breath. "I heard their plans."

He realized then what he'd said a moment ago. Damn! He could hardly tell her why it was so improbable that Perkins was a supremacist. "What plans?"

Another visible gulp. "They . . . they were uh, talking about . . . discussing how to . . . I don't know how to put this."

Kane gripped her shoulders, fighting to keep his hold gentle and reassuring. "How they were going to do what?"

She raised her eyes to him, her skin so pale in the moonlight. "How they were going to get rid of all the . . . Indians. And . . . others. Minorities."

The anger and revulsion that shuddered through his body made it next to impossible to keep his words calm and even. For Annie's sake, he tried. "And what did they decide?" he asked. His tone was hardly emotionless. It was the best he could do.

"They argued. Joe wanted to fence off an area of Montana and . . . and move them all there. Sam . . . well, he just wanted to—God, I can't even say it."

"Wait a minute, Annie. These aren't real plans. This is the raving of a bunch of lunatics. They can't have any real hope of accomplishing any of this."

"That's what I made the mistake of thinking. I knew there was no way Sam truly could be involved. I knew there must be a mistake. So, I waited for him in his car."

"You *what*? Wait a minute, did anyone else see you?"

"I'm not sure. I didn't try to hide. I know they weren't aware I had listened in on the meeting. I heard them before I knocked on the door. I was so stunned, I stood there like a dumb animal, listening. Eventually I think I went a little crazy. I mean, this was the man I'd pledged to spend my life with, talking like something . . . evil. Like a monster. I remember thinking that if I could just talk to him, I'd discover it was all some sick joke."

"What happened when he found you in his car?"

"He . . . well, of course he was surprised." Annie shook her head, shifting her focus back to Kane's shirt pocket.

"Was he upset?"

"I don't really remember, I think I sort of barraged him with questions right off. At first he tried to calm me down and assure me everything was okay. He wanted me to get in my car and follow him home, but I wouldn't. I wanted answers." She snorted.

"I got everything but. He pulled the car around the corner to where I had parked, but I wouldn't get out. I kept demanding to know what was going on." She stopped abruptly, as if all the breath in her had suddenly been used up. She slumped heavily against his chest.

Kane propped her chin up with two fingers until

she looked at him. "Did he hurt you, Annie? Threaten you?"

She shook her head in a slight movement. Her body was still limp, but she'd begun to shake. She seemed unaware of it, her voice hollow as she continued.

"At first he tried to sweet-talk me, saying he wanted to move the date up . . . But I refused to do that until he talked to me, really talked to me . . . Then he got so angry. I've never seen him like that. He . . . he didn't hit me, but it got very ugly."

A heavy shudder rocked her, bringing Kane's protective instincts to the fore. He tucked her against him, rocking her gently, although he couldn't say who benefited more from the soothing motion.

His mind raced as he felt the tremors in her body—or was it his? He knew she hadn't imagined all this. Her recount had been too visceral. There had to be some explanation. But Kane couldn't see it. It was obvious that Perkins was so desperate to keep this quiet that when he discovered he couldn't control her, he'd tried to have her silenced on a permanent basis. Something she'd said niggled at his brain, but he couldn't make himself concentrate.

Now he did shudder. With revulsion and disgust. "Bastard," he muttered softly. "Bastard!" he shouted.

Annie jumped at his furious blast, then huddled even more closely against him. "I'm sorry," he said quietly, pressing his cheek against her hair and stroking a hand down her back. "So that's when you left him?"

"I'd never seen him like that. His face was so . . . contorted. And his voice . . . He'd always had this even, moderate tone. So low-key. I thought it was so soothing. Nothing seemed to ruffle him. He prided himself on always being in control. He liked to control." She laughed. It was a vacant, hollow sound. "Lord knows he controlled me, and I didn't even realize it."

"Don't say any more. It's—"

"I used to envy him that," she broke in, as if unaware he'd spoken. "I wished I could be so steady, so confident. It was one of the reasons I agreed to marry him."

"Annie—"

"But that night, that night his voice was so . . . cold." She shivered, Kane knew she was deep in the memory of that evening three months ago. "He was almost . . . manic. He did threaten me I guess, but I still didn't really believe he'd hurt me. I mean, people use expressions like 'I'll kill you' all the time. I didn't take it literally."

"Annie, stop—"

But she didn't. He knew she had to get through this, once she'd started to purge herself of this ugliness she had to keep on until it was all gone. He hated it. Hated that he couldn't take on this burden for her.

"I figured I'd move out for a while. Let him

settle down. Maybe see if he'd agree to go to a ther-
apist or something." She shook her head, again the
sound of her empty laugh echoed across the lawn.
"Lord, I was so naive. I can't believe I actually
thought—"

"Annie, of course you didn't think he'd really
want you dead. No one could fault you for that. It's
not wrong to put your trust and complete faith in
the man you take for your husband."

"Oh God, and to think how close I came . . ."
she said distantly. Then, more strongly, she added,
"But I should have seen. I didn't . . . that is, my
feelings for him weren't that—" She broke off suddenly, then in a fervent whisper said, "I used to
wonder what he saw in me. Why he'd gone after me
at all. I didn't travel in his circles. We met at a
church function, and he made it his business to become a part of my life almost immediately. It was
flattering and overwhelming. Now I realize he'd
probably purposely looked for someone like me.
Someone he could impress, someone he thought he
could mold into his vision of a perfect corporate
wife. All his suggestions and casual comments . . ."

Kane didn't try to make sense of her jerky confession. He could barely take it all in. One sickening
truth *had* wormed its way into his brain. And now
that he'd given it a moment's thought, he knew at a
gut level that he was right.

*"Find my wife, and I'll make sure you never want
for anything in your life."*

Perkins's words on the day he'd hired him echoed through Kane's mind. At the time he'd thought the man was being expansive about the wealth he commanded, a man used to dangling the enticement of money to get whatever he wanted.

In your life. He'd had a man tail Kane out of town. A hired killer. Probably the same one he'd sicced on Annie. Perkins had never had any intention of letting Kane have a life. Perkins was every bit the monster Annie said he was. What he wasn't was stupid. Kane realized he could take Annie back right now and shout all over town that Sam Perkins was an unbalanced racist. Who would the town believe? Their pure-as-snow local bank president? Or a scorned wife and the half-breed she'd been living with out in the middle of nowhere? An Indian that the supposed racist had hired.

"We need proof he tried to have you killed," Kane said, only half aware he'd spoken the thought out loud.

"Don't you think I thought of that? And even if I had proof, who would I have taken it to? Half of Hunnicutt was at Joe's house that night, many of them powerful people. I have no idea who else is in on it."

Kane moved his hand down to cup her neck, tilting her head back. He locked his gaze on hers, willing her to believe with his eyes as much as his words in what he was about to say. "We'll get him, *Da'bEntcotc.* He won't get away with this."

A soft smile twitched at the corners of her mouth. Her lips were softly swollen, as if she'd been biting them during her confession. The moonlight made her eyes appear the decadent shade of the darkest of chocolates.

"I like it when you call me that, whatever it means."

Kane's body tightened. Her soft voice was like a warm balm against nerves battered by the night's revelations. "It means 'little sun.'"

She lifted a hand to rake through her bright, tangled curls. "I'm not really a redhead, you know." She let out a soft laugh. "As a matter of fact, I'm probably the only woman on earth with blond roots."

Kane felt himself tighten in an entirely different way at the return of the warmth to her voice. "Red or blond, I wouldn't care. That's not why I call you that."

"Why then?"

One quiet request, and whatever restraint he'd held on to through her exhausting recitation slipped through his grasp. He hardly gave it a thought as he slowly twined a strand of her hair around his finger. As if time no longer had meaning, he lightly traced the soft curl along the side of her jaw and down her throat. He let his eyes follow the motion, drawing the long burnished strand down over her T-shirt, to where her chest was pressed against his. He pressed the fiery tendril against his heart, then reached for her hand, placing it on top. "Do you feel that?"

He knew his pulse raced beneath her hand. There was no denying that she felt it.

"Yes," she whispered.

"You look at me, smile at me, even yell at me. And every time, this is what happens." He placed his hand over hers, then lifted it to his jaw. Locking his gaze on hers, he pressed his cheek to her palm, knowing the bite of his new beard wouldn't abrade her callused skin. He hated that fact, wanted her to be as sensitive to the merest touch of him as he was to her. He watched intently as her pupils dilated under his unwavering stare. Lord, she was something. "Smile for me."

A short look of surprise crossed her face, but then slowly, like a new dawn or a freshly blossoming flower, her lips curved for him, then parted to show beautiful white shiny teeth. "That. That's why I call you 'little sun.' "

Her smile faltered. She held it for him, even as a single tear formed in the corner of one eye and slowly made its way down her cheek.

"Sweet Jesus, Annie, don't," he said in a raspy voice.

"I can't help it." She sniffed.

Kane steeled himself against the need to lower his mouth to hers, to taste her smile, to drink in the sunshine that poured from her soul and shone so brightly on his dark one. Giving him hope.

False hope.

"I don't know what to say."

Slowly, he set her away from him. "Say good night," he answered roughly.

Her eyes widened a bit at his brusque request,

but her smile remained. New and now somehow shy. It melted what was left of his heart.

"Good night, Hawk."

Need for her knifed through him so hotly, he fought against bending double to stem it. He had to get the hell away from her before he did something neither one of them would ever forgive him for.

"It's been a long night," he said, his voice so hoarse, it sounded like gravel. "Sleep late tomorrow."

"Okay." Her voice sounded a bit uncertain as she slowly disentangled herself from his lap. "I'll see you in the morning?"

Kane had moved several steps away, but the soft vulnerability lacing her question made him turn around. He choked down the moan that rose in his throat. She looked so damn small and alone. He hated the uncertainty in her voice, but he didn't dare risk even one step in her direction right now.

"We'll talk more after you've gotten some rest."

"Okay." She paused as if about to say something else, then let herself in the back door.

Kane stood and stared through the rusted screen until the soft muted light of the propane lamp glowed from inside the kitchen.

He headed toward the bunkhouse, then abruptly altered his direction to the barn instead. Grabbing a fistful of black mane, he leapt quietly onto Sky Dancer's bare back. Using the subtle pressure of his knees, he steered her carefully down the road leading to the stream, once again glad that the big bay had night eyes almost as good as his. And she never forgot a trail.

He reached a hand down and stroked the mare's neck. She responded with a low rumbling whinny.

"What am I going to do, old girl? Hmm?"

The horse plodded onward, as silent as her rider.

Elizabeth groaned as she stood. She cast a baleful stare at the full bucket at her feet, trying to work up some enthusiasm to pick it up. She rubbed the small of her back and flexed her knees. The sudden sounds of repetitive banging brought her head up, and she turned to look at the barn in the distance.

Kane was back. She couldn't see him from across the field, but she knew the clanging sounds were hammering and were likely coming from the barn.

What she didn't know was where the hell he'd been.

Angry all of a sudden, she turned away, scanning the bramble patch she'd just picked clean. She'd found it earlier that morning when, after a night spent wrestling with her sheets—and her heart—she'd left the house for a mind-clearing walk. She'd watched Kane leave on horseback from her window the night before. He and Sky Dancer were nowhere to be seen when she'd left earlier that morning.

When she'd returned from her walk, she'd found Sky Dancer in the paddock, but still no sign of Kane. She'd even worked up the courage to check the bunkhouse, knowing she might well find him asleep in bed. But other than his gear piled in one corner, the building was empty.

Feeling suddenly confused and unsure, she'd grabbed a bucket and lit out to collect the sweet plump berries from the new cache she'd discovered.

Now he was back. Anger warred with an irritating, overwhelming sense of relief. How dare he wander off?

A moan slipped through her gritted teeth as she lifted the heavy bucket and started across the field. How dare he indeed, she mocked herself. "You're lucky he didn't saddle up and take off at a full gallop the moment you said the word 'supremacist,'" she muttered. Swallowing the sudden sense of dread that clawed at her throat, she pinned her gaze on the ranch house and picked up her pace.

She'd intended to go directly inside and take care of the berries before confronting him, but halfway across the yard, a movement caught her attention.

She sucked in a sudden deep breath and stopped in her tracks. Kane was on the roof of the barn, on his knees, his powerful arms at work tearing up a piece of sheet metal. The motion put into play all of his well-defined muscles, holding her in a sort of thrall. He'd tied his long hair back in what looked like a piece of leather. The jeans he wore were faded and fit snugly against his thighs and . . . She gulped as she spied the split in the worn fabric just below the portion of his anatomy she'd been gawking at.

Even from this distance, she could see her first impression the day she'd met him had been correct. He was the same even brown shade all over.

She could have sworn she hadn't made a sound, but Kane stopped suddenly and shifted around to face her, sitting with his arms resting on his bent knees.

"Hi." His voice carried easily down to her.

Oh my, she thought, not handling the front view any better than she had the back. She set the buckets on the ground beside her. Apparently she'd underestimated her success in using a long walk and hours of mind-numbing work to clear her head.

"Where have you been?" she blurted out, frustrated by the seesawing emotions he always seemed to bring about in her.

"Wait there a minute," was his only response.

With an animal grace she knew shouldn't surprise her, he moved quickly to the edge of the roof closest to the ground. Without a sound, he flipped easily onto his stomach and slid off the side, until he hung by his fingertips. He dropped into a light crouch, straightened, and brushed himself off as he walked toward her.

Her mouth felt as if she'd licked the dust off of him. She couldn't swallow, much less breathe. All she could think of as he drew closer was that she'd cuddled against that very chest the night before, had felt with her own hand the heart that beat so strongly under that dusty bronzed skin.

"You okay?"

His voice sounded rough to her, probably because she barely heard him above the thundering rush of blood pounding in her ears. His concerned expression was what finally grabbed her attention, and she felt the skin on her neck and cheeks heat as she wondered what he made of her obvious reaction to him.

"Yeah, I'm fine." She cleared her throat quietly and shifted her gaze to a point past his shoulder. She wanted to ask him again where he'd gone, where he'd been all morning, but suddenly she felt as if it weren't really any of her business. And she didn't think she could stand hearing him affirm that fact.

She lifted her gaze to the barn roof and kept it there, reverting to the one topic she did have the right to question him on. "I didn't know you were going to work on the roof. Is it bad?"

"Not as bad as I'd expected. A couple of the sheets on one side are rusted, so I'm going to rip them up and switch them with better ones that cover the part of the barn we aren't repairing."

We. A tiny little word. Two letters. It was ridiculous that it should have an effect. Ridiculous and dangerous. She shifted her weight and cleared her throat again. "Good. Well, I have berries to rinse." She bent down, and lifted the buckets. "I'd better be—"

"Annie, stop." Kane raised a hand as if he meant to take her arm, but she took an automatic step out of his reach. The flicker of surprise—and hurt?—

that crossed his face made her flinch, but she didn't move closer. She didn't trust herself where he was concerned right now. The previous night seemed like light-years ago. Now she couldn't imagine being held in his arms. Not without wanting him to—

"I really need to get back to work," she said, fighting to keep her voice even.

"What we really need is to talk."

Anger flared in her, mercifully relieving her of the sudden excruciating awareness of him, of what he was coming to mean to her. "I was out here this morning first thing, but you were nowhere to be found. I couldn't waste the entire day waiting for you to decide to show up." She looked away, dismally wishing she'd been able to control her temper.

"I'm sorry."

His quiet tone jerked her head around. "Where did you go? I was . . . I worried."

She noticed his hands clench into fists at his sides, and she wondered if he'd wanted to reach for her again. She fought the heat that loosened her muscles, making her want to shift closer to him, to reach for him first.

"It . . . couldn't be helped."

Something else was flickering in his eyes now, something she couldn't put a label on. "Why?"

He ran a swift assessing look around them, scanning the fringes of her property with an efficiency that made a chill race down her spine.

"Hawk?" she queried softly. "What's wrong?"

Sky Dancer whinnied from the barn, and Kane went completely still. "I want you to go inside the house and stay there, okay?"

This time she was unable to tamp down the cold fear that sliced through her. "Tell me what's wrong."

"Not now. Just go in the house. I'm . . . let me wash up, and I'll come in and we'll finish our talk."

Instinctively she reached for his arm before he could turn away. "Tell me," she demanded, her voice hushed as his had been. His skin was dusty and hot under her fingers, she could feel his pulse pounding steadily in the ridged vein of his bicep. Her senses vibrated as if the beat were inside her instead of under her fingertips.

She barely had time to process the thought before he turned back and took both of her arms in his hands.

"Do you trust me, Annie?" His gaze was forceful, unwavering.

"I want to."

"Do as I asked," he said, his expression shuttered again. "Please," he added, surprising her. "I'll explain everything as soon as I get back."

She tightened her hold, his bicep twitching in response to her touch. "Get back? From where?" She hated the sound of panic in her voice, but there was no help for it. "Don't go," she begged without knowing exactly why. His eyes darkened, something she hadn't thought possible. He looked the savage now, fierce and indomitable. Tremors rocked her, and this time they were her own.

"I'll keep you safe, little sun." He turned her toward the house. "Go."

She whirled around to tell him it wasn't her safety she was concerned about, but he was racing on sure, light feet across the ground toward the barn. "Be careful," she whispered, then turned and did as he'd asked.

She knew she'd only been in the house for thirty minutes, but she felt as if she'd lived two lifetimes. She relived every nuance of her most recent encounter with Kane, damning herself for her preoccupation with his effect on her. What had she missed? Why had he left the night before and again that morning? Was it related to whatever he was doing now?

She knew darn well he wasn't washing up. She pressed a fist against the cold knot of fear that had settled in the pit of her belly. It was impossible to ignore the possibility that Sam had somehow tracked her down.

"Dear Lord, what have I gotten him into?" She berated herself again for telling him, for giving in to her fear and loneliness and hiring him in the first place. She should have pushed on alone until Matt showed up.

Her nerves tightened painfully, and she shot up

out of the chair and began pacing, careful to stay away from the windows.

There was no point belaboring her latest lapse in good judgment. What was done was done. She'd be better off using the time to beat some sense into her head regarding her feelings for Kane. She'd examined them enough over the last twenty-four hours to know they weren't simply a result of his role in her predicament. Yes, he was strong and honest and made her feel safe for the first time in months.

But he also called to a place deep inside of her. He had an emptiness about him, a sort of hollowness that had an affect on her she was finding increasingly impossible to ignore. The urge to reach out, to find out if she could be the one to fill it was unbearably tempting.

Even if Sam Perkins ceased to exist that very moment, taking her fear for her life with him, she knew she'd go on wanting Kane Hawthorne. Eyes of the Hawk.

As if her wanting had conjured him, he was there. He'd entered through the front door and was coming silently down the short hall when she looked up and gasped.

"What happened?" She ran to him, placing shaking fingers on the thin gash slicing down the side of his temple.

Kane lifted two fingers to his temple, half surprised when he encountered the sticky warmth of his own blood. He wiped his hand on his jeans and took her arm, leading her back to the kitchen.

"I'm all right," he said, steering her calmly but quickly toward the table. He motioned with his head for her to take a seat. He moved to one side of the back door.

"At least let me clean it up a little. If you caught it on a nail or barbed wire—"

He turned from studying the back field long enough to shoot her a crooked grin. "Afraid it will get infected and I'll lose my head?"

He watched her lips curve in response and thought she might even laugh. That's why he'd said it. The tension was a live thing between them. It would help if he could lessen it. Not that it would make what he had to tell her any easier.

Something of what he felt must have shown on his face, because her smile slipped, strain again haunting her beautiful brown eyes.

The night before, Kane had fought back the killing anger he'd hoped to come to terms with, along with his growing feelings for Annie, by taking a long dip in the frigid stream. Instead he'd found something that only served to heighten both emotions.

"Okay," she said, a slight wobble the only indication she wasn't as calm as she wanted him to believe. "If you won't let me play nurse, then will you please tell me what has you standing at my back door like a sentinel waiting to alert the troops of an impending attack?"

He swung his head sharply back to hers, scan-

ning her expression for a sign that she knew something he didn't. All he saw was honest curiosity,
along with a healthy dose of fear.

He forced an even tone as he said, "How about
we pack a quick supper and take a short hike? I
found a spot about a hundred yards above the spring
that would give us front row seats for the sunset."
Not to mention provide him with a hawk's-eye view
of the ranch.

Annie snorted and pushed up from the table,
coming straight at him.

She poked a finger square in the middle of the
T-shirt he'd retrieved from the barn during his
quick inspection of the grounds.

"If you think you can make me spill my guts,
then walk away"—she jabbed again—"come wandering back when you feel like it"—another jab—
"order me into my house while you go off God
knows where, only to sneak in my front door fifteen
minutes later with blood running down the side of
your face, and then expect me to believe you want to
go on a nice little picnic with me"—another poke—
"then your head wound is more serious than you
think."

EIGHT

Kane was worried for her life, fighting the over-whelming urge to kill her husband, not to mention the almost unbearable need he had to hold her. Yet he stood there actually suppressing a smile at her spitfire of a tirade.

His lips quirked up no matter how he tried to keep them flat. "Thank you for caring about me."

Her eyes widened as he'd known they would, he was half disappointed that smoke didn't pour from her lovely freckled nose.

"Care?" she sputtered. "Of course I care! What do you take me for? Someone's trying to kill me and you run off, and I don't know if you've gotten hurt, or maybe you decided to leave or—" In the span of a heartbeat he watched her go from blazing fury to the brink of tears. He reached for her but her palm flattened on his chest, keeping the slight but important space between them.

She sniffed, and her bottom lip trembled as she looked up at him, fury still somehow burning brightly in her glassy eyes. "Dammit, now I'm crying again, and I swore last night I wouldn't do that anymore."

Her shoulders jerked as she sniffed, and all Kane's good intentions flew out the window. "Come here," he whispered, pulling her taut frame against his chest. He pushed the fingers of one hand through her wild red curls, cupping her head, forcing it gently but firmly to his chest. He wrapped his other arm around her waist.

If she'd remained hard and unyielding, resisted him for even a minute, he'd have been able to regroup and let her go. But in the next instant, she relaxed. She didn't cry or sob as he'd expected. She huddled against him, an occasional tremor racking her shoulders, not holding him or otherwise encouraging him, using his arms as a shelter from her internal storm as she slowly pieced together her control.

He damned himself for the bastard he was that she could continue to maintain grace under incredible pressure, while he'd caved in to his base desires on the first sight of tears. Because while she took a well-deserved time-out, he burned with a need to take her, to pull her underneath him and bury himself in her fire and light. Again. And again.

He felt her draw herself together and move slightly away from him. He let his hands drop, then he fell heavily into a chair, not caring if it splintered under his weight, hoping like hell she'd been too preoccupied to notice the state he'd been in. Was still in.

She sat across from him, resting her elbows on the table. "You found something last night." She didn't make it a question so he didn't bother answering her. "Do we need to get out of here for a while? Is that why you suggested the picnic?"

He looked up, letting his respect for her shine in his eyes. "Little sun, when you pull yourself together, you don't waste time."

She sucked in a small breath. "I don't have much to waste, do I?"

He exhaled harshly, flattening his palms on the scarred table. "I don't know. And to answer your other question, yeah, if we're going to talk, I'd like to do it where I can keep an eye on the place."

"Okay. Give me a few minutes to pack something." The look on her face as she cast a glance at the cabinets told him eating wasn't high on her preferred agenda at the moment. But she stood and started gathering things anyway.

"Just like that?"

She turned back to him, her expression leaving no doubt she understood what he'd asked. "Just like that."

Knowing he should stay seated didn't keep him from rising and crossing the small room. He came to stand behind her, wanting to touch her again but somehow finding enough strength at the last second not to. "I'll do everything I can to make sure your faith in me isn't misplaced."

She paused for a split second, then reached for the wooden bowl holding several shiny red apples. "I know."

Two words. Entrusting him with the most precious thing she had to risk; her life. He vowed then and there not to lose control again, no matter the temptation, to do whatever it took to free her of the monster she'd married then get the hell out of her life and let her get on with rebuilding it. Because no matter how badly he was tempted to try and keep her with him, he had nothing to offer her and even less of a reason to give her hope that that fact would ever change.

"Is it safe to climb the rocks above the spring?"

Her words jerked him to the present. Steeling his resolve, he focused completely on the events of the evening ahead. "The barn will block us until we get into the trees a bit farther up."

"And getting past the barn?"

Her voice was remarkably even, but he didn't miss the light trembling in her fingers as she stuffed a box of crackers into the basket.

"Clear." *For now, anyway.*

She turned suddenly, surprising him into complete stillness. "Is that how you got this?" she asked, gently touching the skin next to the gash he'd forgotten about.

He hadn't expected his resolve to be tested so quickly nor so strongly, especially with something as innocent as concern for a little scratch. He forced himself to withstand her soft touch as if it were some sort of test he had to pass before he could go on. It took far more will than he'd thought he had left. "Yeah. I'll stop and clean it out at the spring, okay, Nightingale?"

She smiled. "Okay, Rambo."

She might as well have cleaned out his wound with the salt in the stoneware cellar sitting on the counter. The pain would have been easier to withstand than dealing with the simple yet complex gift of her caring and easy humor at a time when he couldn't tell her how much they meant to him.

Loose rocks skittered down the path behind them as they made the last turn. Kane held a branch out of the way and motioned for Annie to pass him. The track was old and narrow and required concentration, a sprained ankle being the least of the consequences if they didn't.

Kane grimaced as he watched Annie's jeans tighten across her trim backside as she bent and used her hands to pull herself up onto the rocky ledge. He was damn lucky he hadn't broken his neck.

He maneuvered carefully around her, and in a short time cleared a small area of rubble and mountain debris, then stood back as she spread the blanket.

He let her go about unpacking, knowing she was

no more eager to eat than he was, but wanting to put off for a few more moments their inevitable discussion.

"Why don't you start while I get this together."

He should have known she wouldn't play it by his rules. He supposed he should be grateful she hadn't followed him earlier, but he couldn't lie to himself that the rush he'd felt when she'd come down the hall toward him had been one of relief.

"Where did you go last night?"

He swallowed a sigh. "I decided to take Sky Dancer out for a while. I needed to think."

She nodded, and he was glad there would be no pretense of misunderstanding between them.

"Isn't that dangerous? Taking a horse out in the dark?"

"Depends on the horse. But I was going someplace familiar. She never forgets a trail."

"Familiar?"

"The stream."

Again she nodded, and he wondered if she was remembering their fishing expedition.

"Did you . . . come to any decisions?"

"My intention had been to think through all you'd said and come up with a plan of action." *Not to mention take a nice long dip to keep me from coming back, on my knees if necessary, and crawling right into bed after you,* he added silently.

"But?"

"The moon chose an opportune moment to stop playing hide-and-seek, and I noticed something on the ground." He dropped the stick he'd been using to draw patterns in the rock dust and looked up at her. "Tracks. A man, about six feet. Thin, I'd say."

Her eyes widened. "You could tell all of that from a few footprints? In the dark?"

"You'd be surprised what the size and pressure of a print reveals. I went back up on foot this morning and scouted around. I found some tire tracks, small tread, probably a rental car, sedan anyway. They were at the last wide bend in the road down the mountain. I followed the foot tracks from there to the stream."

"Anything . . . closer?"

"No."

She took a small breath and turned back to the basket. After staring at it for a moment as if trying to remember what she was doing, she shifted on her heels and gave up all pretense of laying out a picnic lunch.

"But if whoever it was found the stream, then he must know about the ranch."

"Could be a fisherman looking for an unspoiled stream."

"Driving a sedan? Not likely around here. Besides, most sportsmen stop in at Dobs's store. I don't think he'd have sent anyone up here. I think he suspects I'm not here for a pleasure trip."

"He sent me."

Her eyes met his, all soft and brown—and scared. "I know. And I'm sorry, Kane. Sorry I got you involved in this."

"Don't, Annie. I got myself involved."

"What did . . . ? Did Dobs say something that made you decide to come here?"

"No," he answered, feeling like a lying bastard even though it was the truth. But it was all the truth he could give her. For now. Maybe for always. He'd have to rely on his actions speaking for him. It was the only way she'd trust him enough to let him get the job done. After that, it didn't make much difference what she thought of him. The result would be the same. She'd go her way, and he his.

She studied him for a moment, and he found himself praying she didn't probe that point much further, he wasn't sure he had any capacity left to tell her an outright lie.

"Well, now that you know the entire story, I won't hold you to your promise." She held up a hand to forestall his interruption. "I know you honor your word. But I'm releasing you from it. You had no way of knowing you'd be risking your life."

He felt her lean forward when he shifted his gaze to the rustic tableau of the ranch spread out below them. He tightened his resolve to remain still if she touched him, but wasn't able to actually move away and eliminate the possibility.

"Besides," she went on, mercifully keeping her hands to herself, "Matt should be home soon. He'll help. He has all kinds of contacts. If anyone—"

She broke off on a swift intake of breath as Kane shot to his knees before her. He grabbed her shoulders. "You don't have the luxury of waiting anymore, Annie. I'm all you've got."

He hated the cold fear that filled her wide eyes with an intensity that rocked him. He wanted to erase forever that hunted look. *Prey.* Dobs's description of her flicked through his mind. Not if he could help it.

"I can't let you—"

"You don't have a choice, Annie." His grip gentled, and he absently let his hands run down her arms. Twining his large blunt fingers through her smaller, more slender ones, he squeezed gently. "I want to get this guy, too, Annie. It's personal now."

Understanding dawned in her eyes. "I can imagine how hard it is for you, finding out about this group and knowing who's responsible for perpetuating that sort of garbage. But Hawk, he's dangerous. I didn't get to hear much, but even what I did hear was enough to convince me that they are well organized and not hurting for money. Or power." She grasped his forearms. "Let Matt help me with this. It's not your crusade."

A million emotions crowded his brain, not the least of which was the way his heart dropped to his knees each time she called him Hawk. He didn't bother to elaborate on the reasons this situation had become personal to him. Her assumption wasn't wrong, just not completely right.

"I agree that Matt would be a welcome sight right now, but he's not here and someone else is. In the meantime, we can't just sit here and wait like sitting ducks."

He watched as she fought down the fear that had become an instinctive part of her life, her gaze skittering away as the fear began to win.

Kane's pulse pounded with fury at his inability to put an immediate end to her terror.

"I'll have to leave here," she whispered. She lifted her eyes to his. "I . . . I don't know where to go. And how will Matt find me?"

"Annie—"

"No, Kane. You've done enough. I'll figure something out. No!" she repeated when he tried to cut in. "You've alerted me to the danger here, but now you have to go. I know how angry you must be, how insulted by what Sam's involved in. But it's precisely because of his beliefs that I think you should go."

"I can handle Sam."

"You don't know him."

Kane flinched, feeling again the twist of pain in his gut for having to continue evading the issue of his damning connection to Sam Perkins.

"If he's not worried about killing me, he sure won't think twice about killing you," she stated evenly.

"And I said I was willing to take that chance. I won't leave you here."

Fire lit the depths of her brown eyes. "Why?" she asked, her voice anguished. "And don't give me all that stuff about being the kind of man who can't walk away. Damn your honor and damn your integrity!" she choked out. "I'm barely able to manage here, wondering from one minute to the next when Sam or one of his pals will track me down." She turned pleading eyes to him. "I can't worry about you too."

Kane wondered if a person could hear his heart break. "So don't," he said quietly, wishing more than anything he was worth her anguish and concern. Especially given the harsh truth that all he was liable to do was add to it. "Let me worry about me."

"I don't think I have that choice. Not anymore." Almost to herself, she added, "I'm not sure I ever did."

Kane swore under his breath, his control so close to shattering, he trembled with the effort to piece the ragged edges back together. This was alien territory for him, having someone be truly concerned about him, and frankly, it was scary as hell.

"Little sun," he whispered, his tone rough. "Don't waste that precious energy on me. I've taken care of myself for so long, I wouldn't know what to do with it."

A sad smile lit the corners of her mouth. "That's right, the man with the empty soul. Your black *mu'gua*. If there was ever a soul worth caring about, it is yours, Eyes of the Hawk."

Kane's control snapped like a fine wire tightened past all endurance. Her solemn avowal unleashed a response in him that was elemental, primitive. He untangled one hand from hers, barely registering the tremors in his fingers as he threaded them into her tangle of curls until he could grip her head.

Slowly, so slowly he could feel each complete second tick by, he tilted her head back. Spending his last shred of sanity, he searched her eyes for . . . what? Uncertainty? Fear? Yes, anything to keep him from answering the need that had spiraled out of control the moment she'd spoken his Shoshone name.

It wasn't there.

All he found, amazingly, impossibly, was a need that matched his own. He lowered his head, the blood rushing through his veins, becoming a tangible feeling. He watched the pulse under the soft skin of her temple match his own internal rhythm.

"Stop me." His lips touched hers.

"No." And she lifted her mouth to his.

The first taste of her sweet, warm breath stilled him for the space of a heartbeat. Then she ran the tip of her tongue over his lower lip, and he lost it.

With a rumbling sound that originated deep in his chest, he wrapped his arm around her waist. He slid his other hand down to her nape as he shifted his mouth and deepened the kiss.

She tasted better, sweeter, wilder than even his most tortured fantasies. He pushed his tongue past her soft, wet lips, seeking her tongue, twining with it, drinking from it. The pleasure was so intense, it was almost painful. Then she touched him, framed his face with her hands, slid her fingers into his hair. She slowly worked her fingers against his scalp, she pushed the leather strip holding his hair downward then off. His sanity followed the same path.

"Little sun," he said against her cheek as he pulled in air. No longer consciously guiding his actions, he trailed his lips across her cheek, then down the side of her neck.

"Yes," she responded, arching into him.

His hips bucked forward, his action completely instinctive. He trailed his mouth over the hot surface of her skin, testing the softness of her earlobe with his teeth. He rimmed her ear with his tongue, whispering to her in his own language, knowing from her immediate response that even that was no barrier to how completely she understood him.

She let her hands drop to his shoulders, clinging there for a minute, the sweet bite of her short nails through his T-shirt, making him feel alive. Wildly alive.

He pulled her shirt loose, suddenly overwhelmed with the need to feel her bare skin under his hand. He let his fingers climb the ridge of her spine, memorizing each and every deceptively fragile bone, until the bunching of her shirt prevented him from going farther.

Consumed by the need to explore, frustrated at this flimsy obstruction, he acted on instinct. With a quick yank the woven fabric gave, and he pulled until the shirt split in two as cleanly as if he'd unzipped it.

He heard her gasp as the air touched her bare

back. He swiftly moved his lips from her ear and swallowed the soft sound into his mouth. He kissed her deeply, relentlessly, while his hands took their time mapping the fine muscles that flexed underneath her skin as she writhed in his embrace.

The sound of fabric ripping and the air hitting his own suddenly bare back hit him like a cold shock. But instead of dousing the fire, it fanned it to a white heat. It quickly became a contest to see who could rip the clothes from the other first.

Her shirt flew seconds before his, and when the burgeoning tips of her breasts kissed his chest, he lost any and all capacity to breathe. He stilled completely, wanting to savor this heady rush, to freeze the sensation in time until it was forever a part of his sensory memory.

He heard nothing beyond the pounding of his heart and the harsh gasp of their combined efforts to draw in much-needed air. In that moment, their gazes locked again. Kane felt an instant of fear at the sudden tidal wave of feelings that crashed against his heart.

He couldn't move, could barely breathe. He didn't care. She took one of his hands in hers and raised it to her lips. She turned it over then lowered her gaze to study it. She dipped her head and brushed a light kiss over one knuckle, then another, and another. Then she found each scar, and he knew there were many, and kissed them too. Only when she'd found and healed with her own fiery brand every visible scar, did she take his hand and lower it, laying it against her heart. She held it tightly as if in fear he might yank it back.

And it took will he'd never dreamed he still possessed not to do so. Her gift to him was unbearable —and incredibly, wrenchingly unacceptable.

He'd thought nothing could penetrate the haze of desire he'd been in, nothing except burying himself to the hilt inside her until stopping no longer mattered.

A strange burning made him press his eyelids shut, breaking the formidable bond she'd tried to forge. "You can't do this." His voice was so hoarse, it was barely intelligible.

"I did. I would again."

"It's wrong." He barely swallowed the bile that rose in his throat. Of all the deceptions, this lie to himself became the harshest to endure.

"Look at me."

He obeyed her soft plea instantly. This was his punishment, he thought. Looking into her eyes, eyes that pledged things he never dared hoped for.

Even now. Especially now.

"This isn't . . . It's the hardest . . . thing . . ." He wrapped his arms around her, tucking her against his chest, steeling himself for the further punishment of enduring the feel of her bare torso pressed to his. He buried his face in her hair, having to spare himself the torture of looking at her while he spoke, knowing it was cowardly.

"I'd give anything . . . anything to make things different."

"Different? Than what?"

He dragged air into his lungs and forced the words out. "Than this, than—"

"I know the timing is horrible," she broke in, her words raspy. "I wish it were different too."

"That's only part of it, Annie." He paused for a moment. "You don't love him anymore, you told me that."

He felt her tense and damned himself for thrusting the ugly specter of Sam Perkins between them, but there was no help for it.

"I don't." She tilted her head back, and he looked down into her worried gaze. "There is nothing left for me there."

"You're running scared, Annie. And rightfully so." He stared hard at her, willing her to understand, to accept what he was trying to tell her. "But I'm not your answer."

Color washed into her cheeks, and she tried to pull away from him, flailing one arm out to grope for at least a remnant of her shirt as if her nakedness had suddenly become a point of shame.

Anger flared in him at her obvious misinterpretation, anger at himself for being so callous, anger at her for not having a stronger sense of self-worth. And a rage that was palpable for the bastard who had robbed her of that.

He pulled her around, held her arms tightly in

his hands. "You . . . are . . . everything . . . Everything any man could want, little sun. Never doubt that."

Her shoulders straightened as she locked her gaze with his. "Any man? I don't want any man." She wrenched her arms from his grasp and grabbed at her shirt. She yanked it on so the rip was in the front, swiftly tying it into a knot below her breasts.

Kane couldn't have moved if she'd thrown a lit stick of dynamite at him. She was magnificent. A true glimpse of the fiery nature that lay beneath the shell of fear and doubt that she'd been forced to adopt in order to survive.

"You say my doubts about myself aren't warranted. Did it ever occur to you that your doubts about yourself aren't either?"

Kane shot to his feet in one fluid motion. He was so close, a deep breath would have caused his chest to touch hers. "I know what I have to offer you, Annie. Nothing. Less than nothing. Certainly not what you deserve."

"Since when did I lose the right to be my own judge?"

"Since the night you discovered your husband is a racist," he shot back, hating himself for his harshness. "When you get out of this, when you can put this—him—behind you, then you can be your own judge. But I know that when you finally have that choice, that your choice will not be me."

The fist she'd pressed against her lips during his

speech dropped away. Kane had expected tears, yelling, screaming, at the very least an argument. So he was totally unprepared for her choked sound of relief, much less the tentative smile that curved her lips.

She shifted forward, closing the yawning quarter-inch gap between them. "Is that what this is all about? I can't believe I didn't figure it out. It's my fault, I suppose, for not making it clear."

She'd caught him so off guard, he could almost ignore the tiny electric shocks the brush of her body against his had ignited. Almost. She looked . . . confident. *That's what you wanted, right?* his inner voice taunted him. Yeah, right. He swallowed hard. Twice. "Mak—" He cleared his throat. "Making what clear?"

"Let me ask you something?"

Giving up completely any hope of regaining control of the conversation, he responded on a pained note. "Sure, why the hell not?"

"If I *was* free to choose any man I wanted . . ."

Uh-oh. "Yes?" was all he managed to get out.

"Would you at least give me—us—a chance?" She faltered for a brief moment, and he wondered if his reaction was so obvious. "If I chose you?" she finished on a whisper.

Why was she doing this? "It's a moot point, Annie."

She placed her fingertips on his lips and shook her head. "Hawk, I was engaged. But I'm not—and never have been—married."

"That can't be . . . Sam—"

"Was my fiancé," she finished.

"You . . . lived together?"

He looked shell-shocked. Given what he'd believed, she shouldn't be surprised. But there was something else under the surface of confusion: A trace more disbelief than she'd thought to see.

"Yes. He sort of swept me off my feet, he can be very focused when he wants something." Like her, dead. She shuddered. Shaking that off, she added, "But it was sort of overwhelming and . . . I won't lie and say I wasn't flattered or influenced by all the attention. By his seeming sincerity." She felt her skin burn. "But I wouldn't commit to a wedding date right away. I could barely breathe, much less . . . Anyway, about three months before this happened, Sam finally convinced me to move in with him. He was pushing me to quit my job too. He wanted to give me the chance to see how the house staff was run. Let me learn the ropes, so to speak, of what's expected of a bank president's wife."

She saw the question in his eyes. Part of her felt relieved that he wasn't demanding to know the gritty details, that he respected her past as being her business and not part of what was between them.

There was another part of her, though, the part that had seen how vulnerable this tough man was, how little he trusted others with even the smallest piece of himself. She suspected she'd been given more than most. That part of her wanted to tell him, show him, how special a man he was. And not stop until he believed it.

The choice was taken from her when a high-piercing whinny ripped through the peaceful late-afternoon air.

NINE

Before Elizabeth could so much as jump, she was facedown on the ground, held there by a firm hand at her back. Oddly, her first thought was that this wasn't exactly how she'd imagined him flattening her. She craned her neck awkwardly and saw Kane in a half crouch over her, using the scraggly shrubs that lined the edge of the ledge for cover as he scanned the grounds below them.

Not for the first time she wondered exactly what he'd done over the years to instill such a strong awareness of his surroundings. She'd chalked it up to his background, the instinctive responses and intuitiveness possibly due to his early years on the reservation. Now she wasn't so sure.

She pushed that aside as well. The bottom line was that no matter his past, no matter how unwise it was, she'd entrusted him with her safety. Her life. Judging from the strain radiating from his every pore and the echo of that horrible single scream from Sky Dancer still ringing in her ears, she suspected she just might be putting that faith to the test very soon.

"Kane?" she whispered as softly as she could.

He immediately bent low, pressing his lips to her ear. "Nothing. I don't know what spooked her. I can't see her from here."

Elizabeth tensed. "Is she—?"

"I'm not sure. She could be behind the barn. The paddock she was in is partially blocked." He took his hand from her back, but remained almost prone beside her. "Stay here until I signal you to come down."

"But—"

"Do it, Annie." He paused, then a harsh whisper filled her ear. "You said earlier you couldn't afford to worry for me." Another short pause. "I can't for you either. Promise me that you'll stay here until I come back or signal."

Stunned by the fierceness of his plea, she was slow to answer.

"Promise me!"

She shifted slightly until she could look him square in the face. "Okay! But I'm not helpless." She swallowed against the denial that shone in his eyes. "This is *my* life in jeopardy, you can't expect me not to take an active part in protecting it."

He shook his head, his expression one of supreme frustration. "Just keep your word, we'll discuss the rest later."

In a silent second, he disappeared back down the path. Elizabeth pounded the dirt with her fist, then scooted as close as she dared to the overlook. He hadn't made her promise not to keep watch over him.

Kane moved swiftly, finding it harder than usual to keep his mind singularly on the task at hand.

I'm not married. Her words rang over and over through his mind as he picked his way closer to the cover of the barn. He searched his soul desperately for the relief that should have accompanied such an announcement. After all, wasn't that what he'd wanted? Dreamed of? Fantasized about? Beholdened to no one? Free to come to him?

He slipped silently through the opening in the back of the barn where he'd removed several rotting boards. He bit back an oath. The answer was yes. But he was a truly selfish bastard because he wanted more. So much more. For her. For himself. The bitter truth of just how brutally honest he'd been when he'd said he had nothing to offer her burned his throat like acid. There would be no relief, no celebration. Because the outcome hadn't changed. He was a wanderer. A bounty hunter. They had no future.

His eyes quickly adapted to the pre-evening light that cast the barn in deep shadows. He was alone.

Yeah. He was that all right.

Shoving all thoughts from his mind save making sure the grounds were clear and that Annie was safe, he pressed against the front door, then slid outside. He kept his back to the weathered planking as he moved slowly toward the paddock. In the next instant, all hell broke loose.

Another equine scream rent the air, and as swiftly as he covered the remaining space, he was still too late. Bucking and writhing under her rider, Sky Dancer tried desperately to unseat the stranger.

Kane slid his knife from the sheath on his belt, wishing he had the rifle that was in the bunkhouse. Holding the blade, he balanced the weight in his fingers and waited for the exact moment to let it fly. Unseat him and disable him, but keep him alive for questioning. The mental strategy was automatic. The rider wore baggy clothes and a dusty hat crammed low on his head. Kane couldn't make much of an ID, other than that he was tall and slender as Kane had predicted. But he'd bet his life it was the same mercenary who had tailed him out of Boise.

Kane shifted his weight, preparing to throw, but just then the rider brought a stick down hard on Sky Dancer's flanks and the mare shot forward.

With a bloodcurdling whoop, Kane left his cover, fury at the mistreatment of his horse, changing the aim of his throwing arm to dead center. Even as the mare wildly charged the fence at the opposite end of the paddock, her rider turned and leveled a gun on Kane.

Kane crouched just as the report echoed across the ground, then ducked through the rails into the paddock. As he took aim, the horse and rider cleared the fence and went racing across the side field toward a dense stand of trees.

Kane quickly changed course, knowing he had no hope of catching them on foot, but praying that in her frenzy, Sky Dancer would stick with the familiar and take the trail to the stream that lay in the direction they'd fled.

He skirted the front of the house and let loose a string of curses. The truck's tires had been slashed. With pursuit no longer an option, he switched his mind instinctively back to his immediate surroundings. He hadn't had the time to check for additional prints, but he couldn't risk that the stranger had returned alone. He quickly scouted the perimeter of the house, then the interior, before moving to the bunkhouse.

"Dammit!" He sheathed his knife and scooped up his now-empty saddlebag from the corner where he'd stashed it. Some of the contents were strewn across the dusty planked floor, but he didn't bother searching through it. It was obvious the rifle was gone. He flung the bags hard against the opposite wall. The sun was on its descent, there was no way off the mountain, and the only thing he had to keep them safe was a seven-inch knife and his wits.

He swore again. About the only damn thing in the world he had to be thankful for right now was that Annie had stayed out of the line of fire.

That and the fact that she'd had the good sense not to marry the son of a bitch who was trying to kill her.

Because he'd hate like hell to be the one to make her a widow.

Knowing she'd heard the gunshot, Kane bottled his fury and turned his thoughts to getting back up the trail, wondering how much he was going to tell her.

A rustling sound beyond the warped walls stilled him in midstride. Whoever it was, was moving slowly, stealthily. He gave himself a swift mental kick as he moved to a position flat beside the only door. First, he'd obviously missed a track somewhere, and then he'd made enough ruckus in here to alert an army. At this rate he'd be lucky if he kept Annie alive till sundown. Determination and a fierce rush of protectiveness surged through him, putting him on the razor edge of readiness.

Kane made his move the split instant the intruder moved inside the door. In the space of a heartbeat, he'd slammed him against the wall and held him there with an arm across his solar plexus and a shiny, very lethal knife against the pulse on his neck.

Only it wasn't a he.

Adrenaline pumping through him like a locomotive, combined with the instant understanding of what he'd almost done, ripped his control to shreds. The result was a barrage of bilingual swearing that put the fear of the devil in her eyes.

"Dammit, Annie!" he yelled finally, then still unable to regain control, he buried his knife deep in the wood a foot above her head. He removed his arm from her chest and pinned her to the wall by her wrists, pushing his nose straight up against hers. "You promised to stay put."

She gulped. Several times. Her eyes were wider than he'd ever seen. Her chest barely moved as she fought to draw in a shallow breath.

He wasn't having that problem. His heart was fighting its way out of his chest while his lungs were yanking air in. Trying and failing to calm down, he slid her hands upward until he could hold them over her head in one hand. With the other he gripped her chin. He knew he was scaring her very badly, but dammit . . . ! Very slowly, his voice barely more than a ragged growl, he said, "I could have slit your throat."

"I'm . . . sorry." Her voice was a croak of sound.

"Sorry?" His tone was pure hard steel.

"I heard . . . the gunshot." She shuddered. "The barn blocked my view." Her eyes reflected the wild anxiety she'd experienced, but he didn't move.

"So you crept around the building, making enough noise to alert the dead." Now he shuddered. "What if it hadn't been me in here? Huh? Did you stop to think you might have walked in on the man your fiancé sent up here to kill you?"

Another tremor rippled through her. "I couldn't wait," was all she said. She gulped again, her voice taking on a slight quaver. "I had to know if you were okay," she ended on a whisper.

"Well, I'm not."

Her eyes widened farther, although with apprehension of an entirely different sort. "You were . . . The bullet—?"

"No bullet. Just a woman who can't keep a promise, taking years off my life by almost ending hers. At my hands. Dammit, Annie." His words ended on a ragged whisper. He was still breathing hard, but the edge of his fury was wearing off.

"I tried. I meant to. But after the gunshot . . . I couldn't wait up there forever. I'm sorry I scared you." Her voice faltered. "I'm sorry," she whispered.

His anger fled, but the intensity mounted. It hit him all at once. Her body pinned between his bare chest and the wall. Her breasts brushing his damp skin now as she drew deeper breaths. Her brown eyes staring at him as if in that moment, he was her entire world, her only focus.

His body leapt in response.

Then it changed for her too. He saw it first in her eyes. The trepidation and apology were slowly erased by the dawning of keen awareness. Awareness of the unique disadvantages of her position. And of the equally unique advantages of his.

His blood pressure surged upward again along with another part of his anatomy, when he saw the flicker of excitement dance in her eyes as the dangerous edge they were walking on beckoned to her, erotic and tempting. His pulse shattered its earlier speed the instant her lips parted on a soft moan as temptation became acceptance.

All rational thought fled. Primordial. Visceral. Basic. That was the level he was operating on now.

Keeping her wrists pinned to the wall with one hand, he reached over her head and yanked the knife from the wall. He held it between them, the blade reflecting a glittering silver in the black centers of her eyes.

"Do you trust me, Annie?"

She dipped her chin. "Yes," she whispered.

He rested the flat edge of the blade tip on the bridge of her nose. "Still?"

"Yes."

He slowly traced the blade down her nose, letting it rest briefly on the plump center of her lower lip, exerting the slightest pressure. Her lips parted. He moved the blade to her chin, down to the hollow at the base of her throat.

"And now?"

"Yes." The word was raw, hoarse.

He lowered his gaze and trailed the shiny shaft between her breasts, the enticing crevice made deeper by the knotted T-shirt she wore. "Then why didn't you stay up there, where I knew you were safe?"

He felt the shivers racing through her vibrate the blade. He held very still.

"I thought you were hurt."

Kane wedged the tip of the blade into the knotted fabric tied beneath her breasts. He risked a glance back to her face. Her eyes flared with a sensual heat that rocked him, and pulsing just below the surface was frustration. "I don't underestimate you, little sun. There is a time for instinct, even for reckless behavior." He pushed the knife deeper into the knot. "But there is also a time when I have to be able to count on you to do as I ask."

A slight smile curved his lips. He knew how she felt. His frustration stemmed from the same unmet need.

"I know." Her breathing was becoming more erratic, the pulse in her throat fairly vibrated the soft skin covering it. Yet she held his gaze, not flinching, not moving, the light in her eyes not receding one damn bit.

Sweet Lord, how he wanted her. Needed her.

He flipped the knife suddenly, and the knot shredded. He saw her fight the instinctive inhalation as her breasts were freed from the T-shirt's restraint. The torn edges draped over her sharply defined nipples, the ends hanging limply against her stomach. She didn't move.

"I'm trying to protect you. Risking my life for it." He stabbed the knife back into the wood over her head, and released her hands. Pressing his hands on the wall on either side of her face, he leaned closer to her, so their lips were barely a breath apart. "You say you trust me, little sun."

He felt tremors begin to rock him too. His will to see this through close to disintegrating. He let his gaze drift from her eyes down to her lips, then back up. "I need to be able to trust you too."

Elizabeth felt as if he'd welded her to the wall, the heat in his eyes was so intense. His concentration on her was profoundly ardent, so much so that she only now realized her hands were still pressed to the rough wood above her head. "You can," she whispered. "You can, Hawk."

Her lips parted in anticipation of feeling his mouth on hers. Lord knew the coil of need he'd aroused in her had gone from exquisite to downright violent. A low moan tore from her throat when she realized he wasn't done with her yet. His lips hovered just above hers. He didn't kiss her. He kept his hands flat against the rough planking as he moved closer, crowding her tightly to the wall, pinning her hips beneath his thighs, pressing his own into her belly. His arousal was full and hard.

"Say it again, *Da'bEntcotc.* Little sun, say my name."

"Eyes of the Hawk."

He groaned, his hips bucking against her, and she thought he would surely take her mouth then. A sound somewhere between a cry and a whimper escaped her throat when he did not.

"What's wrong, little sun?" he demanded, his voice low and provoking.

"You're killing me."

He shifted, rubbing his chest back and forth just enough to peel the shirt from her breasts. The sudden feel of his smooth, hot flesh against her painfully swollen nipples made her moan loudly.

Then it hit her. He was stronger, far more powerful than she, could easily take what she was so obviously ready and willing to give. But he didn't. He had her so aroused, it had taken her a while to figure out why.

She let her hands drop to his shoulders. Another low groan rumbled in his chest, barely escaping his tightly compressed lips. Encouraged, she moved her fingers slowly over the deep, rounded contours of his muscles. He shivered as her fingers slipped into the silky black hair that lay long against his neck. She moaned and dug her fingers deeper into his hair until she could grip his head between her hands.

His eyes blazed so hot, she thought she would catch flame, his rigid arousal twitched and throbbed, rubbing the denim of his jeans against her belly. Otherwise he kept utterly still. She could feel his sweat trickle down the center of his chest and into the crease formed by her breasts. She could smell the musky scent of him.

Elizabeth had never felt so alive, so completely aware of her body, her senses, her sensuality. And the knowledge that Kane was experiencing the same thing was intoxicating. His self-restraint had forced them to a point of such heightened sensitivity, she wasn't sure she'd survive it. Nothing in her life had ever come close to this. But then, she'd never known a man like Hawk.

Her grip tightened, and she slowly brought his

mouth down to hers. The first touch of his lips was electrifying, like a thousand bolts of energy zapping each and every nerve ending. She teased him with her tongue, pushing it just inside his mouth then retreating. He didn't follow her lead, simply went on letting her kiss him.

That only served to heighten her desire to an even greater pitch. She thrust her tongue deeply into his mouth, twining it with his, dancing with it, flirting with it, demanding that he respond to her.

"Hawk," she pleaded against his lips when he still refused to take the initiative.

"What?"

"Kiss me back, damn you." She was past being shy. Past worrying about how she sounded. She knew damn well he wanted her as fiercely as she wanted him. "You told me there was a time for reckless behavior," she ground out. "Well, if this isn't that time, I don't know what is."

He pulled against her grip, moving his head just far enough away to look into her eyes. Shockingly, he smiled. A full smile, a devilishly wicked smile.

"Oh, I'd say you're being far more reckless than you realize right now." His smile faded, desire crowding out any last trace of humor. "I just wanted you to understand that everything—trust, desire, power, vulnerability—it all goes both ways between us."

His quietly spoken words zeroed straight to her heart. She looked deeply into his eyes, trying to see if his soul was reflected there, knowing it made no difference any longer. She loved this man. Her dark warrior with a heart that deserved to be cherished.

"Oh, yes," she whispered. "I understand."

"Good."

Elizabeth moved in the same instant Kane did, his hands dove into her hair, hers framed his face. She met his lips halfway across the breath of space between them. They joined fiercely, roughly. Softly, wetly. She took his tongue into her mouth and bathed it with her own, he pulled it back then took hers, pulling on it, drinking from it.

She writhed against him, the ache between her legs overwhelming her, screaming at her for release. She pushed against him, glad for his weight pressing on her, knowing if he stepped away now, she'd slide to the floor in a boneless heap. He moved his hands down to her shoulders, then leaned away so he could cup her breasts.

She cried out when he rubbed a callused thumb over her engorged nipple, then again when his mouth and tongue followed. He teased and soothed one while his fingers tortured the other until she thought she'd explode.

Suddenly he grabbed her shoulders and lifted her up the wall. When he pressed against her again, she felt him hard, heavy and throbbing. It was excruciating, it was exquisite. Instinct guided her, and she immediately wrapped her legs around his waist. He groaned into her hair and rocked against her. Her face was buried in his neck and when his body began to establish a steady rhythm she sunk her teeth into the tight skin stretched across his shoulder.

He didn't even flinch, but she was barely aware of anything at this point except the overwhelming need to remove the barriers preventing them from completing what they'd begun, to put out the inferno they'd started or go up in flames with it. Something, anything, or she was going to die.

"Hold on to me," he commanded, swallowing her positive response in another heated kiss.

She locked her ankles behind his back. He grabbed her hips and pulled her against him as he turned away from the wall and stumbled to the bed behind them.

He sat down so she was in his lap, never once letting his lips leave hers. He ran his hands up her back and down her arms, peeling the tattered remnants of her shirt from her body. Then he pushed her back. "Let me look at you." His voice was raw, barely intelligible.

The light had grown dim, but she could plainly see—and feel—how arousing her nakedness was to him. Her response was innate. She reached up and cupped her breasts in her hands, even daring to let her fingertips brush provocatively over her nipples.

"Sweet God, you're incredible," he intoned, then continued to talk to her, telling her what she made him feel, at some point slipping into his native tongue.

She understood it all, there was no mistaking his

meaning. She reached for his hands and placed them on her, then let go to caress him as well.

He drew his hands up to her face, framing her cheeks. "I need you. Beneath me, over me, through me. With me. No threats of the past, no promises of tomorrow. We know only here, control only what happens between us now."

Elizabeth felt a sharp stinging behind her eyes. She wanted desperately to tell him she loved him, wipe the doubt from his mind, make him believe in the power they shared only together. Except she knew he would believe it was her agitated state of arousal talking.

Instead she let everything she felt for him shine in her eyes as she repeated his words back to him. "I need you too. Beneath me, over me, inside me. No threats of the past . . ." she paused, but couldn't force the rest out. Because she couldn't lie to him. "If you want nothing from me past today, Hawk, I will grant you that freedom. But I won't lie to you, because if I have any control over tomorrow, I will try to make it as special as today."

A great shudder ripped through him, and he yanked her to him, burying his face against her neck as he wrapped his arms around her. She thought she felt a hot warmth on her shoulder, but she didn't have time to think about it, because in the next instant she was flat on her back and they were clawing each other's pants off.

In the tumult, they rolled from the bunk to the floor. Kane cushioning her with his big, hard body.

She gasped as her legs tangled with his, his bold erection thrusting between her newly bared legs. He moved swiftly onto the pile of mangled cotton and denim they'd just discarded. "Annie—"

"Yes!" She tried to shift under him to ease the fierce ache clawing at her, but couldn't.

"Slow—I . . . need . . . to . . ." His words ended in a harsh gasp as she arched under him.

She was beyond comprehending his words, only that she had to have him inside her. Now.

"Sweet mother of—" His rough words were broken off as he groped for his pants, which were pinned under her shoulder, struggling briefly, cursing loudly, then finally freeing his wallet from the back pocket.

Kane barely managed to protect himself before Elizabeth was tugging at his shoulders, pulling his hips into the cradle of hers. The tip of him nudged her, and she buried her face against his chest; kissing him, licking him, biting him.

"Hawk," she panted, wrapping her legs around his hips.

"Little sun," he responded, then thrust into her, fully and completely.

She sunk her fingers into his back, immediately moving against him, pushing as hard, arching as high as she could, unable to get enough of him.

He shook, his forearms showing the strain as he locked them into place above her shoulders. Then he released a mighty groan and began to move, faster, harder. Deeper with every thrust.

Elizabeth met his every stroke, her own cries becoming louder and louder. The pressure built higher, faster, tighter until she screamed with it.

He kissed her, swallowing her screams into his throat, giving her back a few of his as he continued the relentless pace they both demanded.

Then he suddenly shifted his weight back. Gripping her hips, keeping them joined, he moved to his knees, resting his weight on his heels.

"Look at me!"

Her eyes flew open, she hadn't even remembered shutting them.

"Almost there, little sun."

Pinning her with his hot black gaze, never breaking the steady pounding rhythm, he slipped one hand from her hip and let it slide into the tangle of blond curls at the juncture of her thighs where his flesh met hers. He pushed his thumb against her, and she bucked wildly.

"Yeah, come apart for me. For me."

And she did. Like a million fireworks exploding simultaneously, she climaxed, clenching him tightly with spasms that rocked her over and over.

He reached for her shoulders, pulling her up to him and wrapping his arms around her to hold her tight to his chest.

"Hold me," he rasped against the hair tangled at her temple. And with her legs and arms locked tightly around him, his lips open on hers, he came apart in her. For her.

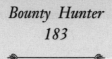

Kane opened his eyes for the second time since Annie had fallen asleep in his arms. Judging by the slant of the moonlight coming through the small bunkhouse window, it was past midnight. Her breathing was deep and steady as it had been several hours earlier when he'd woken and lifted her to the cot. When she didn't awaken, he'd slipped outside to run a quick check on the grounds. No new tracks.

He lifted a hand to the wild tangle of red curls that lay across his chest, smiling when he tried to picture her with hair the same shade of blond as the other sweet nest of curls. He'd thought about moving her—them—to the main house, but she was sleeping so soundly when he'd returned from his little mission, he'd been unable to resist sliding back under the thin blanket and wrapping himself around the warmth of her body. She'd curled right into him, and he'd fallen asleep without even realizing it. Until now.

His hands absently loosened one curl, then another, untangling them, then twining one around his finger. What in the hell was he going to do now? To say things were different was a laughable understatement. Only he wasn't laughing. Never in his wildest dreams had he come close to imagining their joining would be so powerful, so consuming. The idea of walking away from her seemed beyond impossible now. He'd just found her, dammit.

As he lay there breathing in her soft, sweet

scent, he realized he was trying to figure out a way to make it work between them. Even though he knew it was a fantasy. He couldn't imagine her adapting to his lifestyle, and he wasn't so far gone he could kid himself about trying to settle down in one place. What would he do? He knew only one thing; tracking people down. Hardly the sort of life Annie deserved.

Not that it made any difference. The second she found out why he'd come up there in the first place, about his connection to Sam Perkins . . . His stomach pitched.

As much as he'd like to keep her in this narrow, lumpy cot of a bed for about three days, he knew other forces were at work, and they didn't give a damn about his time schedule. He had to tell her now.

"Hawk?" Her voice was a drowsy murmur against his skin.

He'd never get tired of hearing her say that. Despite his recent decision, his body responded as if the other agenda was still a possibility. A frown creased his brow as he wondered whether he'd ever hear her whisper his nickname again after he confessed. He shoved a hand under his head and tugged her a bit closer to his side. "What?"

"Mmmmmm," was all she said.

He could feel her smile against his skin. The hand behind his head became a clenched fist. "Annie, we have to talk."

TEN

She roused herself enough to lay her hand on his chest and prop her chin on the back of it. "About Perkins and the man who shot at you. I know."

At least she didn't sound any happier about the abrupt return to reality than he did. He drank in how naturally they had awakened to each other, as if they'd been doing it every morning for years. His stomach knotted with pain as he fought the need to tell her what that meant to him, how powerful their union was to him. But he knew—as she surely did—that there was no time for that.

"I slipped out earlier. No new prints."

"And Sky Dancer?"

His muscles clenched along with his jaw. "No sign," he muttered. "But I hadn't expected there to be." He let his gaze drift to the tiny window, then he shifted so he could see her face. He pulled in a breath, then forced it out. No time like the present.

"Did you ever go back to Fort Hall? I mean since your grandmother died? Don't you miss having a home to go to?" she asked.

"What?" He'd been all prepared for his big confession, and her off-the-wall question took him completely by surprise. "Where did that come from?"

"I've been wondering why you made the choices you did. Why you took to wandering and never settled down." She laid her cheek on her hand, turning her face away from him. "Never mind, I know it's really none of my business."

He pulled her on top of him so her chin rested square in the middle of his chest. "Ask me whatever you want, little sun."

She smiled, the blush on her cheeks shy and sexy as hell. "Why did you leave?"

He was a little surprised when the pain didn't come. Maybe because she'd tried so hard to hide her curiosity. Didn't she know he could deny her nothing? He actually needed to tell her. It would all lead to the same ending. That he had become a bounty hunter. One most recently employed by a Mr. Samuel Perkins.

He swallowed hard, forcing his mind back to her question. "My mom didn't handle single parenthood well." That was a broad generalization if there ever was one. "She knew my father was never coming back, and that staying on at Fort Hall was her only chance to raise me."

"But that didn't keep her from hating it, did it?"

Kane's chest tightened at her softly spoken words. "No, it didn't."

"Did she . . . spend time with your father in hopes he'd take her away? Marry her or something?"

"More than likely. Cloud Dancer, my grandmother, thought so. I only knew she resented the reservation and hated being pigeonholed as just another Indian. She wanted more. So much more."

"Where is she now?"

"Dead." He felt the shiver that raced through her. "She killed herself when I was six." He took a deep breath, feeling somehow cleansed by the admission. "I didn't understand everything, but I knew she'd have been happier somewhere else." *Without me.* He cleared his throat. "Cloud Dancer tried hard to get me to see that the ways of our culture weren't so bad. But all I knew was that it had been our culture that had taken my mother away from me. I was scared. And ashamed. I knew it was my fault too." He sighed heavily. "I grew up very angry and resentful. I left as soon as I could. I was barely seventeen."

"But you went back once."

"Ten years later. When I found out Cloud Dancer was ill. I was too late. I have no reason to go there again."

Neither of them said anything for a moment, and Kane felt his heart begin to pound. He'd never told a living soul the things he'd willingly confided in her. When she turned her face up to his, he didn't even dare contemplate the emotions he found brimming in her eyes.

"Thank you."

"For what?" he asked, honestly surprised.

"For giving me another part of you. I don't imagine you discuss that part of your life all too often."

"No," he said, his voice gruff. "Annie, there's more. I have to explain what brought me here. What I do for—"

"Shhh!" she said suddenly, placing her hand over his mouth.

He stilled immediately, wondering if he was so far gone with guilt that all his instincts had gone to hell. He heard nothing. "What?"

"I heard something crackling. Wait a minute. Do you smell something?"

"Holy mother of—" Kane sat up, bringing Annie with him, then none too gently deposited her back on the tangle of sheets and blanket. He shot to the window, knowing before he got there what he would find. "The ranch house is on fire."

Annie was on tiptoes behind him, trying to see out the small murky panes of glass. She gasped. "Oh my God—"

Kane turned and pulled her to him. "There's nothing we can do." He wrapped his arms around her and tugged her closer. "I'm sorry, sweetheart. I'm sorry."

All he could think was that if it hadn't been for her sneaking up on him the night before, for them giving in to the emotions that had been building between them since the moment he'd found her kneeling out in the field on those ridiculous sponges, she'd have been asleep in that old feather bed . . . He shuddered against the thought, banishing the mental picture. It hadn't happened, she was okay. For now.

Elizabeth took comfort in Kane's arms for a moment, letting the shock of what was happening and all it implied sink in. Then she got mad. Really mad. She yanked herself away from him. "He's gone too far this time."

Kane let out an incredulous laugh. "This time? Annie, what do you think he was trying to do with the pickup truck? Bump into you? Scare you?" He grabbed her shoulders. "Sweetheart, the man is trying to kill you. And tonight he damn near succeeded!"

"Well, I'm not going to sit here like a scared rabbit and wait for him to finish the job. *I can't sit and wait any longer.*"

"And what do you plan on doing?"

"Face him. Go back. Call the police, the FBI, whoever. Do what I probably should have done in the first place instead of running away."

He shook her. "Annie, it's too late for that. We're trapped. Right now all we can do is keep ourselves alive long enough to find a way off this damn mountain."

She tried to calm down, think rationally. She looked at Kane, at the man she'd just spent the most powerful night of her life with. Talk about life being unfair.

No! Not if she could help it. Not anymore. She'd reached the end of her endurance. It would end now. One way or another, but it would end.

"Kane, I know you want to help me. Lord knows you could have been hurt—even killed—yesterday, when that man fired at you. And your horse is gone . . ." She started to shake. "I can't let you keep—"

"Annie." His tone was a warning.

Her eyes burned. "If anything happened to you . . ." She couldn't finish. In the next instant her face was pressed against his warm bare chest, his hands stroking her back as he spoke into her hair.

"Don't you understand, little sun? It goes both ways. It goes both ways."

There was a sudden crackle and hiss, then a loud crash as a beam or a wall in the old house gave way. Realizing the danger they were still in, Kane set her away from him and tilted her chin up.

"Listen, the house is going up like dry tinder. The propane tank sits far enough away so that it probably won't blow. But the idiot who set the fire could be rigging that to blow right this minute."

"What do you want me to do?" she asked, pushing her hair from her face and swiping at her cheeks.

If he'd doubted it before, he knew it was burned in his soul for eternity now. She stood there, damp cheeks and freckles, slender shoulders shaking but squared, splendidly, beautifully naked while she stared at him and calmly handed him her complete faith. He loved her.

The hell of it was, if the pyromaniac out there didn't get him first, it was likely she'd finish the job when she found out the entire truth. But then, he'd never needed to be told that life wasn't fair. From the very start, his own had been an outstanding example of that.

"I'm going to see if I can find his tracks."

"But what if the tank blows—"

"Get dressed," he interrupted, looking around the small bunkhouse. He scooped up his jeans, sliding his wallet back into his pocket, and stepped into them.

"And then?" she asked as she found her jeans and slipped them on.

He tugged on a dark T-shirt and tossed one of his dark plaid cotton shirts to her. "Do you think you could find your way up that trail? The noise from the fire should cover any sounds you make. Be careful, but move as fast as you can. The fire is lighting up the area as if it were high noon."

"I can do it."

He knew she could. Dammit, they were supposed to have more time. There was still so much he had to say. "Annie—"

"What are you going to do when you find him?"

She sounded so sure of him. Never had he hoped so much that she'd be right. "Depends on what I find." He walked over to the window where she was standing. "Stay up there until it gets light out. If I haven't come for you by then, grab some water from the spring . . ." He stopped long enough to rummage around through the mess on the floor. "Here, take this." He handed her his canteen. "Then I want you to head down to Dobs's. Stay off the road if you can. No need to hurry and don't take any foolish chances." He slid his wallet from the back pocket of his jeans. He fished around and pulled out a bent-up business card, then held it up to the light cast by the fire outside to check the writing on it. "Here. When you get to town, call Brody Donegan."

"Isn't that one of the men I contacted from your list?"

"Yes. Tell him everything. Everything. You understand?"

"Okay, but—"

"No buts this time, little sun. I'd trust Donegan with my life. He'll help you. And he'll help you nail Perkins too. After what you told me yesterday, I was planning on calling him anyway."

"Okay, I will." She paused a beat, looking up at him with a thousand questions in her eyes. "Thank you," was all she said.

"Don't thank me yet." Lord, what a tangled mess his life had become. "Come here," he said softly, feeling incredibly blessed when she moved into his arms without question. He lowered his mouth to hers, needing to taste her, absorb all that was her into him. Knowing that even if they came out of this in one piece, he'd never have her in his arms that way again.

The instant she opened her mouth under his, the sweet tender kiss he'd intended turned into something hot and hungry. Needy and demanding. And from the way she clung to him, held his head tightly in her hands, he wasn't the only one fighting the sudden inferno.

Another roar from outside broke them apart. On a harsh breath, Kane whispered raggedly, "I'll make sure you get past the open area to the edge of the trail." He cupped her chin and kissed her hard and fast. "Wait for me."

He ducked out the door, flattening himself to the wall, not certain, with the rush of sound coming as the house suffered its last death throes that he had heard her quiet response.

"Forever, Hawk."

Forever. Hawk. He cleared his mind and moved to the corner of the bunkhouse, carefully peering around the edge. In the false brightness he quickly scanned the grounds. No one. Without looking behind him, he motioned for her to take off. He spared a quick glance to make sure she was in fact heading for the cover of the trees at the base of the trail. She was hardly more than a dark blur. He swung around and kept his eyes glued to the Dante-esque scenario in front of him, alert for any movement beyond that of the crumbling pile of ash.

❖————————❖

Elizabeth stumbled up the last ten yards of the trail, flopping down as soon as she was behind the shrub cover near the ledge. She could hardly believe she had been there that afternoon. It seemed as if she'd experienced more in the hours since than she had in her entire life.

"Come on, Hawk," she murmured as she flattened onto her belly and shimmied closer to the edge. She found herself half hoping he didn't find anything. She'd gone over his instructions a thousand times while climbing the trail. And as soon as she saw him, she planned to do everything short of kidnapping him to get him to go down the mountain and contact this Donegan person with her.

She had long since come to the conclusion that the situation was far beyond her control. And she knew now that waiting for Matt to show up was a luxury she couldn't—

A hand clamped over her mouth, sending her thoughts flying in a thousand directions and her heart rate soaring. She instinctively began to struggle, knowing without conscious thought that it wasn't Kane's hand. She kicked and thrashed, trying to scream. She managed to get her mouth open a bit and was preparing to bite down, when the man's voice penetrated her haze of self-protective rage.

"Go on and bite me, you little bitch. Ain't nothing gonna stop me now."

Elizabeth's blood ran cold. She turned her head as far as she could—and looked directly into the eyes of her killer.

Her first instinct was to ask what had happened to Kane, but she quickly clamped her lips together. If Kane was hurt or worse . . . there was nothing she could do about it. But in case he wasn't, or her attacker didn't know his whereabouts, she wasn't about to clue him in.

"He's not gonna save you this time. You're mine."

Her confidence in being rescued took a swift nosedive. She forced herself to maintain eye contact, wanting him to think she wasn't intimidated. However, no amount of self-control could keep her limbs from trembling. "Is he . . . ?" She couldn't get past the hoarsely spoken words.

"Dead?" The man laughed. It was a lifeless, menacing sound. He dragged her roughly to her feet, pulling her hard against his body. "Don't much matter. Unless he's halfway to Canada by now, he's as dead as you're gonna be shortly."

He pulled one arm painfully backward, then upward until her fist was between her shoulder blades. She sucked in air as needles of pain shot through her shoulders, fighting the burning behind her eyelids. Think, think! she commanded herself. But her mind wasn't cooperating. Jumbled thoughts of Kane talking to her, kissing her, making love to her seemed to race through her mind simultaneously. Dear God, if she was about to die, then she hoped her killer's words were prophetic and somehow Kane had escaped.

He jerked her arm roughly, and she couldn't

stem the tiny yelp of pain. Shoving her in front of him, he started to move toward the tiny trail leading down from the ledge. She stumbled blindly for several steps then something inside her snapped. *Why am I going along like a sheep to its slaughter?* In the next instant she sprang into action. Putting her weight on her left foot, she stomped down with her right, hoping to catch his shin—and him off guard. She accomplished the first and was rewarded with a bellowed curse. However, when she turned into his body and tried to knee him in the groin, her body tangled with his and they both went tumbling to the ground. She landed on the bottom, and the blow drove the air from her lungs in one big whoosh. Even gasping for breath, she didn't lay still. She squirmed, jerked, fighting and clawing like a wild animal to get free.

"Dammit to hell, lie still."

The shouted curse was immediately followed with a hard backhand to her face.

Her ears were ringing, and she was having a hard time making her eyes focus, but it didn't take more than a second to realize she was staring down the barrel of a rifle. Kane's rifle, she thought dazedly.

"Stupid bitch, we could have had some fun first, but I'll be damned if I'm gonna let you punch and claw me while I'm at it."

"You thought I'd lie still and let you rape me!" she demanded. An idea leapt into her mind, and she instantly gave voice to it. "Sam's paying you, right?

Whatever it is, I'll double it, triple it. I even have contacts that can get you out of here, safe."

He shoved his sweaty stubbled face close to hers, and her stomach lurched at the smell of his foul breath.

"Sam was right in having you silenced. You don't understand anything about what we're doing. You probably been screwin' that half-breed." He shook his head and spat in the dirt next to her cheek. "I ain't doin' this for the money. I'm doin' this because it's the right way."

Any hope she had of bargaining with the man died as she saw the fanatic flair of obsession light his gray eyes. She should have known he was one of Sam's followers. His voice rang with an almost religious fervor.

"You women don't know your place anymore. And your Indian lover, he's only good for tracking, drinking, and sucking money from the government of the U.S. of A. Can't decide which one of ya I'm gonna enjoy doin' more."

Fear escalated to terror. It clawed at her throat, making it impossible to breathe. Was he going to torture her first? His expression was downright demonic as he stared at her. She began to pray for a swift death, murmuring silent prayers to her brother and Kane, apologizing for not being more valiant in the final moments of her life.

She felt the barrel of the rifle press against her temple at the same moment she heard the click of the safety being released. One hot tear escaped her tightly shut eyes.

The shot was so loud, it deafened her.

But it didn't kill her.

In fact, it hadn't hit her at all. Either that or she'd died so instantly, she hadn't felt anything.

Then another sensation filtered through her brain. She'd heard a sound, a high keening cry almost like a bird—or a hawk—just before the rifle had sounded. Her eyes flew open.

"Kane," she whispered in stunned disbelief. She blinked once, then again. He was really there. Only then did she realize she was free to move. She rolled onto her stomach, meaning to push up to her feet, but halted on her knees. The pain arrowed through her head where she'd been struck, causing her to bend forward and brace one hand on the ground. She thought she might even be sick. Fighting the nausea and the stars blinking in her peripheral vision, she tried once again to stand.

"Stay down, Annie."

She turned her head too fast and ended up unintentionally complying. "Kane?" He had her attacker face down in the dirt, his knee planted in the middle of the man's back, holding his head by a fistful of hair. She didn't know what had happened to the rifle. Kane was holding his knife.

"Damn you, Hawthorne," the man ranted. "Get off of me." Kane must have pulled harder, because the man visibly flinched, then swore again. "We're on the same side, ain't we? Sam wanted her found, she's found. Now let me do my—oof." His sentence was cut off when Kane jerked his head roughly backward.

Elizabeth thought his neck might snap. She wondered if the man had gone over the edge of sanity. His words made no sense to her. "Kane, tell me where the rifle landed."

"In the bushes," he jerked his head to his right.

She scrambled on her hands and knees, heedless of the bite of the rough terrain against her palms. She rooted through the bush closest to Kane and his captive. It only took a few seconds to find it. "Here!"

"Just hold on to it. Aim it at the ground."

Elizabeth did as he asked. Something about what her attacker had said niggled at her brain, but before she could grasp it, Kane bent low and began talking to him, drawing her full attention.

His voice was a hiss in the man's ear. "I want your name. Who hired you and why, and where you hid the car. Tell me now, and *maybe* I won't slit your neck."

"Harold Lucheck. Sam Perkins paid me . . . to silence his girlfriend. Car's in the trees . . . about a mile back down the road."

Kane tugged a bit harder on his hair. "Where's my horse?"

"Don't know. Swear. She was gone when I . . . when I got back from torching the house. Thought I tied her tight. Maybe the smoke spooked her."

"You alone?"

"Yes."

Kane didn't react to the information other than to tuck the knife away. "Put your face in the dirt."

Kane could feel the defiance in his tightly clenched muscles.

"What you gonna do, half-breed, scalp me? I told Sam not to hire—"

Kane found only a tiny measure of satisfaction in the crunching sound Lucheck's nose made when he helped him follow instructions. Gripping Lucheck's wrists tightly behind him, Kane dragged the moaning man toward the nearest tree at the beginning of the trail and shoved him down to his knees. He slipped his belt off with one hand and turned the man so his back was to the trunk. "Put your hands behind you around the tree."

"Go to hell," he shot back, but a close-up look at Kane's knife made him comply.

He cinched the man's hands tightly around the trunk, then crouched down and took the bandanna from the man's neck and gagged him.

"Except Perkins, I've never wanted to hurt anyone as badly as I want to hurt you. I'm talking long, slow, and bloody." He stabbed the knife in the ground up tight between the man's legs. "I wouldn't move if I were you."

Kane stood and forced his fists to loosen. The whole episode hadn't taken five minutes. He'd wanted more like five hours with the guy. When he'd first discovered the fresh tracks and found them heading for the trail, his throat closed and his stomach dropped. When he moved into the clearing and saw Lucheck pinning Annie to the ground, a rage filled him so fully that he could barely see through the red haze that clouded his vision.

It had taken considerable restraint not to flay the skin off the man strip by strip. But in the last recess of his brain that still functioned on logic, was the knowledge that this man was their only link to nailing Sam Perkins.

"Kane?"

Annie's voice, rough and hoarse, drew him from his murderous thoughts, and he turned to face her. He had no idea what she was thinking, but she had to have heard Lucheck. She had to know.

Half expecting her to cock the rifle and aim it at his chest, feeling as if he deserved no less, he was surprised when she dropped the rifle instead and launched her body against his.

He instinctively caught her, but instead of pushing her away as he should have, he tightened the hold and buried his nose in her hair.

"I'm sorry, little sun. I'm sorry."

"You got here. I'm alive," she whispered. "You're alive. There's nothing to be sorry about."

She didn't know. Obviously the trauma of the moment had kept Lucheck's damning words from sinking in.

"Annie—" he began, but she cut him off.

"Is it really over?" She looked up at him. "I can't believe it's over." Tears lined her lashes, but her cheeks were dirt streaked and dry.

He saw the red welt swelling her right temple and tensed with a new rush of fury. "He hit you? What else, Annie? Tell me!"

"Nothing. I'm okay."

"Like hell you are!"

Kane made to put her aside, but she grabbed his shirt in her fists and held on tightly. "Don't! Don't leave me," she added. Only the vulnerability in her voice kept him from going straight over to the tree where Lucheck was tied and finishing what he'd started, but with a much more satisfying conclusion.

He stared down at Annie, hating himself for not preventing what had happened to her. "You sure you're okay?" he asked softly. Unable not to, he reached up a finger and very lightly traced the skin near her bruised flesh. "I wanted to kill him, Annie," he whispered. "I still want to kill him."

The tears brimmed over and trickled down the sides of her nose, removing tiny trails of dirt to reveal the freckles that lay underneath. In that moment he wondered if he'd ever be able to look at a freckled nose and not feel his eyes burn with shame.

"I know. I'm not too happy with him either. But he's our link to Sam. You did the right thing. We can get him now. Right?"

He couldn't answer. All he could do was stare at her, wiping her tears away with his blunt fingertips one by one as they fell. He studied her, her beautiful eyes, her freckles, her lips, everything. He took his time. It was going to have to last him the rest of his life.

"Hawk?"

Unthinkingly, he wiped her last tear and put his damp fingertip to his lips. It was a mistake. Tasting her tears unleashed a tidal wave of emotions he didn't dare label. All he knew was that she'd almost died and he had to taste her, feel her alive against his mouth—if not his body—one last time. He would likely roast in hell for it. But then, he'd expected to do that all along anyway.

He meant to make it brief, but one touch of her warm lips undid his resolve. He took her hungrily, over and over. When she met his tongue with a thrust of her own, he thought his tears would surely come, but they remained behind his eyes, burning like the acid that was eating away at his soul. "I shouldn't . . ." he murmured brokenly, "I can't stop," he mouthed against her lips. "Help me to stop, little sun."

Her breathing ragged, she managed to pull back a breath. "I know," she panted. "We need to get him out of here, get the authorities."

Dear God, if it were only that easy, he thought. He knew the pain had only begun for her. He wanted to cut his heart out and hand it to her. It would be simpler than saying what had to be said. Betraying her.

He set her away from him until they no longer touched, stifling the moan that rose in his throat at the severed contact. He wasted a half a second trying to convince himself that what he was about to do was for the best, that no matter how it had started, the ending was inevitable.

"Annie, we need to get to Lucheck's car and get him down to Dobs. I'm going to call Brody and have him set things in motion."

"Let's go then. I want to get out of here." She shivered slightly and rubbed her arms.

Kane clenched his fists. "There's something I have to explain first."

"Can't it wait? I really—"

"No. Listen to me. I've tried to tell you this before. You have to know this." Kane paused and looked over his shoulder at Lucheck. He motioned for Annie to follow him a few yards down the trail, out of earshot. They'd given the bastard enough of a show, he'd be damned if he'd spill his guts in front of the lunatic.

"What is it, Kane?"

He turned to face her. "I don't know how else to tell you this, so I'm going to say it straight out. All I ask is that you let me finish."

"You're scaring me." She folded her arms over her stomach. Kane felt his own clench even tighter.

"I'm not here by accident, little sun. Sam Perkins hired me to find you. I'm a bounty hunter."

ELEVEN

Elizabeth felt the blood drain from her face. No. No! She wanted to scream the words at him. She wanted to clamp her hands over her ears like a child and hum some tuneless song so she couldn't hear him. But there was no avoiding the truth.

She swayed and grabbed onto the trunk of the closest tree for support, trying desperately to make sense out of what he was telling her. Then she recalled Lucheck's words. *"We're on the same side."*

She looked up at him. "Why?" It was only one word, but it was filled with anguish. She took little consolation in seeing the same emotion reflected in his eyes.

"Perkins told me you were his wife and you'd run off after a blowup about money. He was afraid you'd come to some harm."

"Why would he . . . ?" He's lying!" She felt

the hysteria she'd managed to hold at bay overtake her.

"I know, I know."

"When did you know?" she said, her voice rising anyway. "Just what are you planning to do now?" Quickly losing her battle with nerves, she didn't stop to consider what she was saying, just lashed out at him. "Why did you stay? To get me into bed? Are you taking me back to him now?"

Kane grabbed her by the arms and gave her a little shake. "Let me finish, dammit," he said, his voice breaking for the first time.

Elizabeth choked on the hot tears that threatened to fall. She pulled from his grasp and stood perfectly still.

"It took me a while to track you down."

"How did you find me?"

"I searched your brother's apartment. I found the picture of you and Matt taken at the Lazy F."

"But we were just kids!"

"I'd exhausted every other possibility. It was a lead. The Lazy F sign and the mountains in the back gave me a place to start." Kane should have told her he'd taken it, but he didn't. He'd thought to return it eventually, telling himself it was merely evidence in a case. But he knew now that he'd taken it because the image in Perkins's glossy photo hadn't jibed with the photo of the scrawny seven-year-old with pigtails and scuffed knees.

"Why didn't you take me back the day you found me?"

Kane exhaled on a deep sigh. It was such a loaded question. "Because I knew something wasn't right even before then. I was tailed when I left Boise, but I didn't know why. That's the reason I ditched my truck for Sky Dancer. I lost Lucheck just south of Coeur d'Alene." *And then I met you*, he added silently. *And you stood there with your hair all curly wild and red, the sexiest damn freckles sprinkled across your nose, sporting sponges for knee pads. And you stole my heart.*

But he couldn't tell her any of that. It was no excuse for what he'd done, and he wouldn't use something that was so precious to him as a defense.

"Were you afraid this other guy was going to get to me first and take your fee away from you?"

"Never," he said quietly. She'd either have to believe it or not.

"That sure of yourself?"

"The only thing I was sure of was that no spoiled, pampered wife would be doing the back-breaking work you were doing because she was in a snit over money. When you told me the truth, I realized that the man following me had no intention of letting either of us come back."

"Which was why you disappeared that night," she said, more to herself than him. "I'm surprised you believed me at all. I mean, why would a leader of a supremacist group hire someone who wasn't . . . ?"

"White? I guess he figured he'd use me for the only thing he saw me as good for—namely my tracking skills—then dispose of both of us. He's not stupid. He knew that if we somehow turned on him and told our side of the story, it was doubtful anyone would believe the accusations of a scorned girlfriend and a half-breed bounty hunter."

She stared at him for a long moment. "I guess you're right." She waited a few seconds longer, then asked, "Why didn't you tell me all this before? After we . . ."

"Think about it, little sun. I tried. Right before you smelled the fire. There was no time." He held up his hand, certain what her next question would have been. "I couldn't tell you earlier. Answer me this; would you have let me help you if I had?"

She dipped her chin. "No."

"Annie—"

"Why did you? Help me?" She let go of the tree and took a step toward him. "This is your job. So why help me?"

"I could say it was because my life was in jeopardy too. Sam had no intention of letting me collect that fee."

"And would that be the truth?"

"No."

She opened her mouth as if to say something, then shut it. Before he could continue, she stepped by him. "We'd better get down there and find Lucheck's car." She saw Kane glance back at Lucheck. "Should we bring him down now?"

"He isn't going anywhere."

"Fine." She turned and picked her way down the trail.

Kane stood and watched her walk away. Away from him, from all he'd done—both right and wrong—for her. He thought ahead to the call he planned to make. Brody would arrange a transport for Lucheck and set the proceedings into motion to track down Perkins.

He didn't know if he would have a chance to be alone with her long enough to talk again. Or what he would say if he did. He'd done the only thing he could do for her—keep her safe. He had nothing further to offer her. "Damn." He started down the hill. "Damn, damn, damn."

Elizabeth paced across the dirt road toward the tiny Boundary Gap post office, then back toward Dobs's store. She was surprised she hadn't dug a trench by now. Where were the helicopters? She groaned inwardly.

Despite her resolve not to, she looked up the road to where Kane had disappeared in the sedan almost an hour earlier. He'd woken Dobs—who was far less grumpy at being woken up in the wee hours of the morning than she'd have guessed—and placed a call to Brody Donegan. He'd left Lucheck tied up in the post office, then said something about going back to check on the ranch. She had a sneaking suspicion Sky Dancer played a part in his hasty retreat, but he hadn't given her any time to ask.

She shivered, rubbing her arms as she walked into Dobs's store. She knew she should be feeling somewhat vindicated. Kane had told her and Dobs and Letty—who'd made a surprise appearance shortly after Dobs—that by the time they got Lucheck to the authorities, Sam should be in custody. With their testimony and Lucheck's, Sam wouldn't be walking free.

Enough time for her to figure out what the hell she was going to do next? The sound of tires crunching gravel drew her to the screen door. Kane was back. She stepped outside.

"Annie?"

The softly whispered word cracked through the stillness like a whip. She spun around. Kane was leaning against the side of the store.

She fought the urge to rub her arms again, feeling the sudden need to appear calm and collected. This was the first time they'd been alone since their talk on the trail. She said the first thing that came into her mind. "I wish they'd get here."

"They will."

She hated feeling so uncomfortable around him. Uncomfortable in a way she'd never been with him before. It wasn't at all pleasant this time. "Did you find Sky Dancer?"

His eyes widened a fraction, but his expression remained unreadable. "No."

"I'm sorry."

"I am too. But I haven't given up yet. She's a tough old mare. She'll be okay."

Elizabeth didn't question his faith. Somehow she knew he was right. He shifted away from the building suddenly, making her flinch. The grimace that flickered across his features told her he wasn't any more at ease with her than she was with him. Somehow that hurt her even worse.

"Walk with me?" he asked, his tone neither inviting nor intimidating. "I need to talk to you before the chopper gets here."

This was it, she thought, her heart beginning to pound. She nodded and followed him across the lot toward the road. They walked in silence for a while. She glanced over at him. She knew from the tight line of his shoulders that he had something on his mind, but she didn't know what to say to him. So she said nothing.

"I collected my gear," he said without preamble. "I also checked the house. It's still too dark to be certain, but I wouldn't get my hopes up. I'm sorry. I know there were some family things you'd probably liked to have kept."

This time Elizabeth did shiver. His tone was sincere and he was saying all the right words, but there was an underlying flatness in his voice. As if she were no more than an unfortunate victim he'd tried to help and now had to console. She shuddered again as it occurred to her that basically, that description was fairly accurate.

Was that all she really was to him? Had he left a whole string of broken hearts behind him wherever he'd been? It should have made her angry. It made her want to cry.

She pulled in a deep breath to loosen the knot forming in her chest. "You're leaving, aren't you?"

He studied her, then looked away, up at the waning night sky. Several long seconds passed before he looked at her again.

"After I give my statements, yes. I'll be back to search for Sky Dancer, but after that . . ."

"You'll go . . . where? To your next job? Where do you go, Kane? I know I asked you this before. Do you have anywhere to call home?"

Kane felt his chest squeeze tightly. Home. "I have a small apartment in Pocatello. I'm not there much. I . . . it's rented out most of the year." That and a P.O. box, he thought. It had always been enough. He looked at her. The pain intensified. "I don't do well in one place. I don't . . ." He let the sentence drift off unfinished.

"Fit in?"

"Maybe. I'm good at what I do, Annie. It's enough."

"Is it? Is it really?"

He didn't think it was possible to feel worse than he already did. He was wrong. "Don't pity me, Annie. I chose this life. I have no regrets." Except not being the right man for you. If only . . . He shut off that train of thought. It led nowhere. Their time had finally run out.

She shifted her gaze forward, continuing down the path of the road. "I don't know. I'd have said this life chose you, not the other way around. You did the best with what you were given. I don't pity you for that, I admire you. But that doesn't mean you can't—"

"Little sun."

She stopped and immediately looked up at him.

Kane knew she was in no shape to listen to anything more he had to say. But he knew better than she that it was now or never. He trembled with the need to touch her, taste her, just once more, but he didn't dare. He was already asking far too much of her by not walking away without another word.

"No matter what you think of me, I want you to know that once I'd met you, I'd have never hurt you."

"I know that. I think I always knew that. It just . . . I was so unprepared for your . . . confession." She stepped closer to him. "But I know you'd never have hurt me. You risked your life for me."

A sudden rush of sound brought both their heads up. The first helicopter had arrived. Beams of light cut wide paths over the nearly deserted parking area as the large aircraft swooped overhead. It began its descent, aiming at the wide section of road behind them. The noise was so loud, Kane knew she wouldn't be able to hear him.

He reached under his shirt and yanked the leather strip from his neck that he'd tied on back at the bunkhouse. He motioned for her to lift her hair, which was whipping wildly in the windstorm created by the helicopter blades. Leaning forward, he tied it swiftly behind her neck. The small amulet, made of pulverized pine needles wrapped inside a small leather pouch, dangled below her breasts. He scooped it up and warmed it in his palm.

He slid a finger into the neckline of her shirt— his shirt actually—and dropped it inside. He then lifted her hand and placed it over the small lump it made under the soft cotton fabric, leaning down so his mouth was next to her ear.

"To keep you safe, little sun. Always, you will be with me, Eyes of the Hawk," he intoned, repeating it in Shoshone. He pressed a hot, sweet kiss to the pulse at the side of her neck, then turned her toward the men who'd jumped out of the helicopter and were heading toward Dobs's store.

It was past dawn when Kane boarded the first helicopter. They'd both been questioned thoroughly by the two agents and were finally being allowed to leave. He'd offered to go on the first transport, thinking she wouldn't want to ride back with Lucheck. Or with him.

He wasn't certain what her reason had been, but she'd quietly agreed. After determining that Sam had been picked up, Annie had asked if it was all right to go back to her brother's apartment for the time being. Plans had also been implemented to locate and contact Matthew. They'd had no more time for private talk. But then, there was nothing else to say.

Kane stared out the domed front of the helicopter as they lifted off. He saw the second chopper circling in the distance, waiting for them to leave so that it could land. As his helicopter reached enough altitude to head out, the pilot tilted the bird, allowing him one last glance at Annie, standing in the doorway of the store.

"Good-bye, Elizabeth Ann Lawson," he whispered as they moved off toward the distant peaks. "Good-bye, little sun."

TWELVE

Elizabeth dug her heels into the side of the big bay mare, wishing she'd paid more attention to Brody during his incredibly patient attempts to teach her how to ride.

"Come on, old girl, we're almost there." Her words sent white puffs into the crystalline winter air. She patted the horse's neck, wishing she'd trailered the animal up this mountain instead of giving in to her foolishly sentimental idea of riding into Kane's life as he had ridden into hers the summer before. She reached up and tucked behind her ear a lock of once-more blond hair. Then, tugging the brim of her Stetson lower on her forehead, she prayed he wouldn't make her walk back down the mountain when he saw her.

She halted the horse as she crested the next rise on the snow-packed trail. Oh my. Brody hadn't been kidding. The land Kane had purchased three months earlier was definitely a slice of heaven.

She smiled. She hadn't known who'd been more surprised; her at hearing Kane had bought land, or Brody for actually telling her about it. She admitted she didn't have Kane's tracking skills, but for an ex-secretary she wasn't half bad.

She scanned the valley before her. It was stunning. Beautiful wide, open fields, marked only by the skeleton rows of fence posts poking up through the snow and the occasional stand of aspens. The Bitterroot Mountains provided an awe-inspiring backdrop only Mother Nature could have created. Nestled in the middle of it all was a modest log cabin, or at least most of one. There were also several corrals, a large barn, and the framework of several other buildings.

But instead of the hive of activity such construction should warrant, only the sound of a single hammer cut through the cold winter silence.

She prodded the horse and covered the final distance. There was a four-wheel-drive truck parked in front of the main cabin. She looked around. Brody had said Kane mentioned rounding up the horses he had stashed all over Idaho and western Montana, but she didn't see any sign of them. Well, he had one now.

Nerves on edge now that the moment of truth had arrived, she dismounted, biting back the groan at the twinge of protest from her inner thighs. She tied the horse to the railing of the finished front porch. As she'd managed the last stair up, quietly stamping snow from her boots, a loud thwack rang out. It was immediately followed by a string of words that made her smile in a way she hadn't been able to for five long months.

She stepped inside without knocking, leaning on the doorframe. Her breath escaped on a soft whoosh. Dear Lord, she'd missed him. She drank her fill of him. His hair was longer, she thought, though it was hard to tell the way he had it tied back. His flannel shirt was damp from his labors, his chest straining at the worn fabric as he pulled in a deep breath. He was as glorious as she'd remembered. She swallowed against the memories of how close she'd once been to that warm, powerful body. She'd never felt as safe and secure since.

She banished those dangerous thoughts and slid the small ladylike knife—it was only five inches long —from the sheath she had strapped to her belt. With all his swearing and cussing, he still hadn't noticed her. She balanced the weight carefully, then tossed it so that it landed, pointdown, in the piece of wood Kane had just dropped back onto the bench so he could hold his throbbing thumb.

"Might as well cut it off now and save yourself the trouble later."

He went completely still. It was another long, mind-wracking moment before he looked up.

"Annie?"

She nodded, damning the burning sensation that had come from nowhere at the unguarded leap of emotion in his eyes when he'd first seen her. It was gone now, a carefully guarded look in its place. But she'd seen it, and it gave her hope.

"I have something that belongs to you. I brought it back."

"Annie," he repeated, as if still unable to believe she was actually there.

Elizabeth kept talking, not wanting to give him the chance to throw her out yet. "She's a little worse for the wear, you were right, she's a tough old—"

"What are you talking about?"

"Sky Dancer. I found her. With Brody Donegan's help. She was up in the Selkirks. We tracked her after the first snowfall. She was a bit banged up—"

"Is that why you came here? To return my horse?"

She didn't know what she'd expected, but it certainly wasn't the flat, expressionless response she'd gotten. She knew how much that horse had meant to him. Knew he'd almost killed himself trying to find her. It had been her one tie to Brody. She'd been banking on it being her tie to Kane. If she was wrong, then maybe she'd been mistaken about— No. She'd come too far to question her actions now.

"No," she repeated out loud. "You also have something that belongs to me."

He didn't say anything, but she noticed his hands were now tightly clenched into fists.

She knew convincing her dark warrior that he was worth fighting for was going to be tough. The fact that he'd bought land had renewed her hope. She'd been preparing for this showdown for months. Only now did she realize she hadn't known the half of it. Maybe that was just as well.

"What?" The single word seemed to have been forcibly wrenched from somewhere deep inside him. "What do I have of yours?"

So he wasn't as unaffected by her as he seemed to want her to believe. Please Lord, let her be right about this.

She swallowed hard and looked him straight in the eye. "My heart. I gave it to you over five months ago. I came here to find out if you still needed it." She took a deep breath. "If not, then I want it back. I'm—" Her voice broke. "I'm having a hard time going on without it."

He cleared the construction rubble in one graceful leap, and in the next second she was where she'd wanted to be every second of every day since the moment he'd said good-bye.

"Oh God, you feel so good," she said against his wonderfully hard, broad chest. Her tears fell unchecked. Everything she'd kept bottled up inside her for months came tumbling out in one long rush. "I tried to go back to my life after Sam was arrested, after the trial . . ."

She remembered how abandoned she'd felt when Kane's deposition had been read but he hadn't appeared. She looked up at him. "I tried, Hawk, but I . . . I found out I didn't have one." She didn't want to take her hands from his shoulders even long enough to swipe her tears from her cheeks.

As if he'd read her mind, he reached up and rubbed them softly away with his thumb. The tender gesture, even while his expression was still so wary, made her cry even harder. "Nothing I did seemed right. Matt tried to help me. He found an apartment for me, bullied me into looking for a new job. He even tried to find you for me." She sniffed, a watery smile on her lips. "He swore he was going to drag you back and do anything short of killing you to get you to take me off his hands." Her attempt at laughter was a choked failure. "I knew I had to see you again. Matt and I both tried to find you, but we had no luck. I even went to the reservation . . ." Kane's eyes widened in shock, but she kept on, there was no stopping now. "It was fascinating. I learned a lot." Such as how special the amulet was he'd given her and how hard his life must have been as a child, she thought. But they could talk about her experience later. "No one there knew where you were either. Then I remembered Brody Donegan . . ." She looked up at him, "I found his card. I . . . I called him."

"He sent you here?"

"In a manner of speaking." Brody had become her friend and ally in a time when she'd needed both desperately.

"I knew from Dobs that you hadn't found Sky Dancer. I . . . tried to get Brody to tell me where you were. All I found out was that you'd bought this land."

"That was several months ago."

"I know. I sort of struck a bargain with your friend. He's very protective of you."

"What sort of bargain?" He didn't comment on the rest.

"He told me you'd decided to give horse ranching a try. So in exchange for helping him track down Sky Dancer, he'd teach me everything he could about horse ranching."

She'd surprised him with that one. Good.

She hurried to finish her explanation before he could say anything. "Only when I'd proven myself to him—and trust me when I say he's not an easy man to impress—would he tell me where you were."

"How long ago did he tell you?"

Kane's quiet question jerked her thoughts to the present. "Five days."

Again he was silent. Damn the man and his unreadable face. Despite his physical show of welcome, she had no idea what he was thinking. Her nerves were frayed almost past the snapping point.

"You went to all that trouble to find me. Why?"

His expression was one of cautious need, like that of a kid who'd been told Santa really did exist, but was waiting for the proof in case it was all a horrible joke.

"Because the night you said good-bye to me, you didn't let me say good-bye to you."

"Is that why you're here, then? To say good-bye?"

"I'm here to tell you that I love you. The good-bye part is up to you." She held her breath. He didn't exactly look overjoyed.

"Would you say that again?"

She squared her shoulders, locked her rocking knees together, and looked him square in the eyes, pouring everything she had into her words, knowing this was her last chance. "I, Little Sun, love you, Eyes of the Hawk."

The fierce look that entered his eyes should have made her turn tail and run. And she might have if he hadn't yanked her tightly against his body and brought his mouth down to hers for the hardest, longest, sweetest kiss she'd ever experienced.

He took her mouth again and again. It went on and on, and she didn't think she'd ever get enough. Finally they both had to break for air. It was then that she realized she hadn't truly tested her courage. She looked up at him, taking comfort from the fire of desire flaming in his eyes.

It was the other emotion she saw there that had her reaching deep inside for the unwavering faith and trust she had found she still had in him. "You weren't ever planning on coming back for me, were you?"

The pain etched in his face sliced at her. "No."

"You know, I was really angry at you for a long time after you left. But not for the reason you might think. Your role with Sam was the easy part to deal with. Your actions spoke loud enough, and after thinking about it, I understood why you couldn't tell me. What I don't understand is, if we shared something that was as wonderful and unique as I think it was, why didn't you have enough faith in me to let me be part of the decision about any future we might have?"

"Your life was in Boise. Mine . . . I didn't have a life."

"What about this place? The ranch?"

"I didn't plan this. I guess I understand what you went through. I took on several more jobs, but my concentration was shot." He lifted his hand to her face. "I kept seeing brown freckles and hearing this soft laugh." He let his hand drop, soft color blooming on his bronzed cheeks. "I missed you, Annie. Every day."

"Then why—?"

He placed a finger against her lips. "I bought this land as a test. Of myself, of my life and what I had or hadn't done with it." He gazed deeply into her eyes. "I have no idea if I'll last the winter here, much less make a go of this. I might be as miserable staying in one place as I was . . ." His voice drifted off.

"As you were?" she prompted, her heart thrumming at what she swore he'd been about to say.

"As I was without you. But Annie," he added quickly, and she knew her hope had shown plainly on her face. "This"—he gestured around him— "doesn't really change things. I'm still not sure what

I want, where I'm headed." He took her face in his large palms. "I still don't have anything to offer you. Certainly not what you deserve."

"What do I deserve, Kane?" she asked softly, determination lacing her every word. She was fighting for her life. "Do I deserve to be happy?"

"Of course. More than anything, that's what I hoped for you."

"And what about you? Don't you think you've earned the same right? What would it take to make you happy, Hawk?"

"You."

"Then why in the hell are we standing here arguing?"

Frustration and pain lanced through his proud features. "Because, dammit! Haven't you heard a thing I've been saying? I can't promise you anything!"

"Have I asked you for a promise?" she shouted right back. "I don't recall needing a promise before deciding to spend three months of my life learning about ranching because I knew that's what you wanted to do."

"And what if this doesn't pan out? What then, Annie? Don't pin your dreams on me. I'll disappoint you." His anger fled as suddenly as it had appeared. He pulled her into his embrace, and when he spoke, his voice was choked with emotion. "I've barely managed to survive these past five months by telling myself you'd gone back to your life. That you were happy. I don't think I could survive trying, and failing you."

She ran a trembling hand down his face. "But I'm not happy. What you do for a living isn't what made me work so hard to find you. It was a means to an end. It's you, Kane. Whatever you are, wherever you go. It's you that I need to be happy." Her voice broke. "Only you."

Tears brimmed over his thick black lashes. "What did I ever do to deserve someone like you, little sun?"

"You came to me, offered your protection, your support, your shoulder, your friendship. Your life."

"You forgot one thing," he whispered roughly.

"What?"

"My heart, I gave you my heart. I love you, Elizabeth Ann Lawson. I love you, little sun."

Elizabeth jumped up and held on to his shoulders so her face was even with his. "I love you," she whispered fiercely, the words interspersed with kisses on his cheeks and forehead until he lowered her so their mouths fit together.

He kissed her long and hard, soft and sweet. He finally lifted his head so they could both take in some much-needed air. "I will make you a promise."

"I'm not—"

"I want to. I may not do this right, and I can guarantee things won't always be easy. But little sun, I promise I will always, always give you the best that I have in me to give."

"Then that's the very best I could have hoped for. The same goes for me, you know."

"But I'll warn you," he said hoarsely, "I'm new at this. It will probably take me years. Sixty or seventy, at least."

"Wait a minute, I have something else to give you." He lowered her to her feet. The feel of his body rubbing along hers almost made her forget her intention, but she forced her mind back to her purpose.

Reaching inside her blouse, she tugged the leather necklace free. Finally. "I don't think I'll need this to keep me safe any longer."

He took the amulet and stared at it for a long moment, then abruptly lifted her into his arms. He stalked down the hall into a partially completed room that was furnished only with a bed. A very big, very old looking four-poster bed.

"This was Cloud Dancer's. I've had it in storage for so many years . . ." Kane looked down at her again, still truly stunned. For the second time, his life had been turned upside down and changed forever. For the better. Both times it was due to the woman, this woman in his arms, who actually loved him. All of him. Kane Hawthorne. Eyes of the Hawk.

He moved to the top of the bed and draped the amulet over the corner of the only decoration in the entire room—a large silver frame sitting above his headboard.

In it was the picture of her at age seven, standing proudly next to Matt under the Lazy F sign.

On the other corner of the frame hung an exact replica of the necklace he'd given her.

She smiled up at him. "I think maybe you had faith in us all along."

He smiled. The full, sexy, breathtaking smile she'd only seen once before. She decided then and there that she would see it again. Often.

"Maybe you're right. That one belonged to my *bi'a*, my mother. Cloud Dancer made it for her." He nodded at the one he'd just added. "That is the one my *bi'a* made for me."

"Your mother? Oh, Hawk."

He saw the tears trip over her lashes and felt his own eyes burn. "I love you," he whispered.

She reached for him, opening her mouth to his as he lowered her to the bed, then turned and pulled her on top of him. Her weight felt wonderful, perfect, cradled between his hips. His body responded, he was so hard with the need to reclaim his place in her warmth that he wasn't certain he'd make it past removing his clothes.

"Annie," he whispered, then bit down softly on her ear. She squirmed deliciously on him, making him groan. "Last time . . ."

"I know," she said, her voice as breathless as his.

"But this . . . This time, I want to take it slow." He lifted his head and framed her face in his hands. "I want to know every inch of you, little sun. Taste you, touch you."

"Yes. Me too. Every inch of you." She slid her hand down over his chest. "Touch you," she breathed against his lips. "Taste you."

Kane lost control. He closed the distance, sinking his tongue deeply into her mouth. His hands moved over her. All over her.

"To hell with taking it slow," she growled in his ear.

Kane smiled against her lips. "Little sun," he said, "we aren't leaving this room until hunger or thirst drives us out."

"Could take hours."

"I was thinking more like days. Two. Maybe three."

She writhed against him, pulling at his shirt. "Maybe by then we'll have figured out how to do this slowly."

Through clenched teeth he said, "Then again, maybe not."

She reached up and raked her fingers through his hair. "*Tu'pambe*," she murmured silkily.

Kane's chest swelled, and his heart tightened. Lord, it was a lucky man who'd be blessed with hearing the sweet sound of Annie's voice each morning for the rest of his life.

Damn but he'd be forever grateful that man was him.

He suddenly realized what she'd called him. *Tu'pambe*. Shoshone for black hair. He remembered what she'd said earlier. "You really did go to the reservation."

"Mmm-hmm," she mumbled as she started to undo the buttons of his shirt.

"*Waipe*," he said.

"Woman," she responded, as if he was quizzing her.

Unable not to, he whispered, "*Gwu'aho*."

She immediately lifted her head to look into his face. "Wife," she said softly, her eyes bright with hope.

"Another new dream," he admitted roughly. When her eyes turned wary, he tightened his arm around her. "But only until I can find a preacher."

He was rewarded with a fierce kiss, and returned it wholeheartedly. "There's one thing this *tu'pambe* needs to know first."

"Anything."

"I want to know if it's true what they say?"

"About what?"

He raked her curls back into her face, reveling in every scent, taste, and texture that was her. "About blondes having more fun."

She tossed her head back, then slid her toes slowly up his calves. "I'm not certain. But I know a great way to find out."

THE EDITOR'S CORNER

What an irresistible lineup we have for you next month! These terrific romances from four of our most talented authors deliver wonderful heroines and sexy heroes. They are full of passion, fun, and intensity—just what you need to keep warm on those crisp autumn nights.

Starting things off is **ONE ENCHANTED AUTUMN**, LOVESWEPT #710, from supertalented Fayrene Preston, and enchanted is exactly how Matthew Stone feels when he meets the elegant attorney Samantha Elliott. She's the one responsible for introducing his aunt to her new beau, and wary that the beau might be a fortune hunter, Matthew is determined to stop the wedding. Samantha invites Matthew to dinner, sure that seeing the loving couple together will convince the cynical reporter, but she soon finds herself the object of Matthew's own amorous pursuit. Another utterly romantic novel of unexpected passion and exquisite sensuality from Fayrene.

Billie Green is back with **STARWALKER**, LOVESWEPT #711, a unique and sexy romance that'll have you spellbound. Born of two bloods, torn between two worlds, Marcus Aurelius Reed is arrogant, untamed—and the only man who can save Laken Murphy's brother's life. She needs a Comanche shaman to banish an unseen evil, but he refuses to help her, swears the man she seeks no longer exists. Her persistence finally pays off, but the real challenge begins when Laken agrees to share his journey into a savage past. Tempted by this lord of dark secrets, Laken must now trust him with her wild heart. Once more Billie seduces her fans with this enthralling story of true love.

Victoria Leigh gives us a heroine who only wants to be **BLACKTHORNE'S WOMAN**, LOVESWEPT #712. Micah Blackthorne always captures his quarry, but Bethany Corbett will do anything to elude her pursuer and keep her baby safe—risk her life on snowy roads, even draw a gun! But once she understands that he is her only chance for survival, she pleads for a truce and struggles to prove her innocence. Micah refuses to let his desire for the beautiful young mother interfere with his job, but his instincts tell him she is all she claims to be . . . and more. In a world of betrayal and dark desire, only he can command her surrender—and only she can possess his soul. Victoria has created a thrilling tale of heated emotions, racing pulses, and seductive passions that you won't be able to put down.

Please give a big welcome to Elaine Lakso, whose debut novel will have you in **HIGH SPIRITS**,

LOVESWEPT #713. Cody McRae is tall, dark, dangerously unpredictable—and the only man Cass MacFarland has ever loved! Now, six years after he's accused her of betrayal, she is back in town . . . and needs his help to discover if her spooky house is truly haunted. As wickedly handsome as ever, Cody bets Cass he is immune to her charms—but taking his dare might mean getting burned by the flames in his eyes. Funny, outrageous, and shamelessly sexy, this wonderful novel offers spicy suspense and two unforgettable characters whose every encounter strikes romantic sparks.

Happy reading!

With warmest wishes,

Beth de Guzman

Senior Editor

P.S. Don't miss the women's novels coming your way in October. In the blockbuster tradition of Julie Garwood, **THIEF OF HEARTS** by Teresa Medeiros is a captivating historical romance of adventure and triumph; **VIRGIN BRIDE** by Tamara Leigh is an elec-

Don't miss these phenomenal books by
your
favorite Bantam authors

On sale in August:

THE LAST BACHELOR
by Betina Krahn

PRINCE OF WOLVES
by Susan Krinard

WHISPERED LIES
by Christy Cohen

"One of the genre's most creative writers. Her ingenious romances always entertain and leave readers with a warm glow."
—*Romantic Times*

Betina Krahn

THE LAST BACHELOR

Betina Krahn, author of the national bestsellers THE PRINCESS AND THE BARBARIAN and MY WARRIOR'S HEART, is one of the premier names in romance. Now, with this spectacularly entertaining battle of the sexes, her distinctive humor and charm shine brighter than ever.

Antonia's bedroom was a masterpiece of Louis XIV opulence . . . in shades of teal and seafoam and ecru, with touches of gilt, burnt umber, and apricot. Sir Geoffrey had spared no expense to see to her pleasure and her comfort: from the hand-tinted friezes on the ceilings, to the ornate floor-to-ceiling bed, to the thick Aubusson carpets, to the exquisite tile stove, hand-painted with spring flowers, he had imported from Sweden to insure the room would be evenly warm all winter. Every shape, every texture was lush and feminine, meant to delight her eye and satisfy her touch . . . the way her youth and beauty and energy had delighted her aging husband. It was her personal retreat, a balm for her spirits, her sanctuary away from the world.

And Remington Carr had invaded it.

When she arrived breathless at her chamber door, she could see that the heavy brocades at the windows had been gathered back and the south-facing windows had been thrown open to catch the sultry breeze. Her hand-painted and gilded bed was mounded with bare ticking, and her linens, comforters, and counterpane were piled in heaps on the floor around the foot of the bed. It took a moment to locate Remington.

He stood by her dressing table with his back to her, his shirt sleeves rolled up and his vest, cravat, and collar missing. The sight of his long, black-clad legs and his wide, wedge-shaped back sent a distracting shiver through her. When his head bent and his shoulder flexed, she leaned to one side to see what he was doing.

He was holding one of her short black gloves and as she watched, he brought it to his nose, closed his eyes, and breathed in. A moment later, he strolled to the nearby bench, where her shot-silk petticoat and French-cut corset—the purple satin one, covered with black Cluny lace—lay exactly as she had left them the evening before. She looked on, horrified, as he lifted and wiggled the frilly hem of her petticoat, watching the delicate flounces wrap around his wrist. Abandoning that, he ran a speculative hand over the molded cups at the top of her most elegant stays, then dragged his fingers down the front of them to toy with the suspenders that held up her stockings. She could see his smile in profile.

"No garters," he murmured, just loud enough to hear in the quiet.

"Just what do you think you are doing?" she demanded, lurching forward a step before catching herself.

He turned sharply, then relaxed into a heartstopping smile at the sight of her.

"Women's work . . . what else?" he said in insufferably pleasant tones. "I've just given your featherbeds a sound thrashing, and I am waiting for the dust to clear so I can get on with turning your mattresses."

"My mattresses don't need turning, thank you," she charged, her face reddening. "No more than my most personal belongings need plundering. How dare you invade my bedchamber and handle my things?" She was halfway across the room before she realized he wasn't retreating, and that, in fact, the gleam in his eyes intensified as she approached, making it seem that he had been waiting for her. Warnings sounded in her better sense and she halted in the middle of the thick carpet.

"Put those back"—she pointed to the gloves in his hand—"and leave at once."

He raised one eyebrow, then glanced at the dainty black seven-button glove he held. "Only the best Swedish kid, I see. One can always tell Swedish glove leather by the musk that blends so nicely with a woman's own scent. Your scent is roses, isn't it?" He inhaled the glove's scent again and gave her a desirous look. "I do love roses."

He was teasing, flirting with her again . . . the handsome wretch. It was no good appealing to his sense of shame; where women were concerned, he didn't seem to have one. Her only hope, she realized, was to maintain her distance and her composure and use deflating candor to put him in his place. And his place, she told her racing heart, was anywhere *except* the middle of her bedroom.

"You rush headlong from one outrage into another, don't you, your lordship?" she declared, crossing her arms and resisting the hum of excitement rising in her blood. "You haven't the slightest regard for decency or propriety—"

"I do wish you would call me Remington," he said with exaggerated sincerity. "I don't think a first-name-basis would be considered too much familiarity with a man who is about to climb into your bed and turn it upside down." Trailing that flagrant double entendre behind him, he tossed her glove aside and started for the bed.

"Into my . . . ?" Before she could protest, he was indeed climbing up into the middle of her bed, pushing the featherbed to the foot of the bed and seizing the corners of the mattress. As the ropes shifted and groaned and the thick mattress began to roll, she felt a weightless sensation in the pit of her stomach and understood that he was moving more than just a cotton-stuffed ticking. The sight of him in those vulnerable confines was turning her inside out, as well.

"Come down out of there this instant, Remington Carr!" She hurried to the edge of the bed, frantic to get him out of it.

"I have a better idea," he said, shoving to his feet and bracing his legs to remain stable on the springy ropes. "Why don't you come up here? There's plenty of room." He flicked a suggestive look around him, then pinned it on her. "You know, this is a very large bed for a woman who sleeps by herself. How long has it been, Antonia, since you've had your ticking turned?"

A romance of mystery, magic,
and forbidden passion

PRINCE OF WOLVES
by
Susan Krinard

"A brilliantly talented new author."
—*Romantic Times*

*Through with running from the past, Joelle Randall had
come to the rugged Canadian Rockies determined to face
her pain and begin anew. All she needed was a guide to
lead her through the untamed mountain wilderness to the
site where her parents' plane had crashed so long ago. But
the only guide Joelle could find was Luke Gévaudan, a
magnetically attractive loner with the feral grace of a wolf
and eyes that glittered with a savage intensity. She couldn't
know that Luke was the stuff of legends, one of the last
survivors of an ancient race of werewolves . . . a man
whose passion she would not be able to resist—no matter
how terrible the price.*

Joey was too lost in her own musings to immediately
notice the sudden hush that fell over the bar. The
absence of human chatter caught her attention slowly,
and she blinked as she looked around. The noisy
clumps of men were still at their tables, but they

seemed almost frozen in place. Only the television, nearly drowned out before, broke the quiet.

There was a man standing just inside the doorway, as still as all the others, a silhouette in the dim light. It took Joey a moment to realize that he was the focus of this strange and vivid tableau.

Even as the thought registered, someone coughed. It broke the hush like the snap of a twig in a silent forest. The room suddenly swelled again with noise, a relieved blast of sound as things returned to normal.

Joey turned to Maggie.

"What was that all about?" she asked. Maggie was slow to answer, but the moment of gravity was short-lived, and the barkeep smiled again and shook her head.

"Sorry about that. Must have seemed pretty strange, I guess. But he tends to have that effect on people around here."

Joey leaned forward on her elbow, avoiding a wet puddle on the counter. "Who's 'he'?" she demanded, casting a quick glance over her shoulder.

Setting down the mug she'd been polishing, Maggie assumed an indifference Joey was certain she didn't feel. "His name is Luke Gévaudan. He lives some way out of town—up the slope of the valley. Owns a pretty big tract of land to the east."

Joey slewed the stool around to better watch the man, chin cupped in her hand. "I know you've said people here don't much care for outsiders," she remarked, "but you have to admit that was a pretty extreme reaction. . . . Gévaudan, you said. Isn't that a French name?"

"French-Canadian," Maggie corrected.

"So he's one of these . . . French-Canadians? Is

that why the people here don't like him?" She studied Maggie over her shoulder.

"It's not like that," Maggie sighed. "It's hard to explain to someone from outside—I mean, he's strange. People don't trust him, that's all. And as a rule he doesn't make much of an attempt to change that. He keeps to himself."

Unexpectedly intrigued, Joey divided her attention between the object of her curiosity and the redhead. "Don't kid me, Maggie. He may be strange and he may be standoffish, but you can't tell me that wasn't more than just mild distrust a minute ago."

Maggie leaned against the bar and sagged there as if in defeat. "I said it's complicated. I didn't grow up here, so I don't know the whole story, but there are things about the guy that bother people. I hear he was a strange kid." She hesitated. "He's also got a bit of a reputation as a—well, a ladykiller, I guess you could say." She grinned and tossed her red curls. "I'm not sure that's the right word. Let's put it this way—he's been known to attract the ladies, and it's caused a bit of a ruckus now and then."

"Interesting," Joey mused. "If he's so popular with the local women, I can see why the men around here wouldn't be overly amused."

"It's not just local women," Maggie broke in, falling naturally into her usual habit of cozy gossip. "Though there were a couple of incidents—before my time, you understand. But I know there've been a few outsiders who've, shall we say, taken up with him." She gave an insinuating leer. "They all left, every one of them, after a few months. And none of them ever talked."

Wondering when she'd get a clear look at his face, Joey cocked an eye at her friend. "I guess that could make for some resentment. He may be mysterious, but he doesn't sound like a very nice guy to me."

"There you go," Maggie said, pushing herself off the bar. "Consider yourself warned." She winked suggestively. "The way you're staring at him, I'd say you need the warning."

At Joey's start of protest, Maggie sashayed away to serve her customers. Joey was left to muse on what she'd been told. Not that it really mattered, in any case. She wasn't interested in men. There were times when she wondered if she ever would be again. But that just wasn't an issue now. She had far more important things on her mind. . . .

Her thoughts broke off abruptly as the man called Gévaudan turned. There was the briefest hush again, almost imperceptible; if Joey hadn't been so focused on him and what had happened, she might never have noticed. For the first time she could see him clearly as he stepped into the light.

The first impression was of power. It was as if she could see some kind of aura around the man—too strong a feeling to dismiss, as much as it went against the grain. Within a moment Joey had an instinctive grasp of why this Luke Gévaudan had such a peculiar effect on the townspeople. He seemed to be having a similar effect on her.

Her eyes slid up his lithe form, from the commonplace boots and over the snug, faded jeans that molded long, muscular legs. She skipped quickly over his midtorso and took in the expanse of chest and broad shoulders, enhanced rather than hidden by the deep green plaid of his shirt. But it was when she reached his face that the full force of that first impression hit her.

He couldn't have been called handsome—not in

that yuppified modern style represented by the clean-cut models in the ads back home. There was a roughness about him, but not quite the same unpolished coarseness that typified many of the local men. Instead, there was a difference—a uniqueness—that she couldn't quite compare to anyone she'd seen before.

Her unwillingly fascinated gaze traveled over the strong, sharply cut lines of his jaw, along lips that held a hint of reserved mobility in their stillness. His nose was straight and even, the cheekbones high and hard, hollowed underneath with shadow. The hair that fell in tousled shocks over his forehead was mainly dark but liberally shot with gray, especially at the temples. The age this might have suggested was visible nowhere in his face or body, though his bearing announced experience. His stance was lightly poised, alert, almost coiled, like some wary creature from the wilds.

But it wasn't until she reached his eyes that it all coalesced into comprehension. They glowed. She shook her head, not sure what she was seeing. It wasn't a literal glow, she reminded herself with a last grasp at logic, but those eyes shone with their own inner light. They burned—they burned on hers. Her breath caught in her throat. He was staring at her, and for the first time she realized he was returning her examination.

She met his gaze unflinchingly for a long moment. His eyes were pale—and though in the dim light she could not make out the color, she could sense the warm light of amber in their depths. Striking, unusual eyes. Eyes that burned. Eyes that seemed never to blink but held hers in an unnerving, viselike grip. Eyes that seemed hauntingly familiar. . . .

Joey realized she was shaking when she finally

looked away. Her hands were clasped together in her lap, straining against each other with an internal struggle she was suddenly conscious of. Even now she could feel his gaze on her, intense and unwavering, but she resisted the urge to look up and meet it again. The loss of control she'd felt in those brief, endless moments of contact had been as unexpected and frightening as it was inexplicable. She wasn't eager to repeat the experience. But the small, stubborn core of her that demanded control over herself and her surroundings pricked at her without mercy. With a soft curse on an indrawn breath, Joey looked up.

He was gone.

Some secrets are too seductive to keep, and too dangerous to reveal.

WHISPERED LIES
by
Christy Cohen

For thirty-seven years Leah Shaperson had been trapped in a marriage devoid of passion. Then a stranger's tantalizing touch awakened her desires, and she found that she'd do anything to feel wanted once more . . . even submit to reckless games and her lover's darkest fantasies. But she would soon learn that the price of forbidden pleasure is steep. . . .

"I know," Elliot said. His voice was hoarse and the words were garbled.

"What?"

"I said I know," Elliot said, turning to her. He showed her a face she didn't recognize, red with suppressed rage. She clutched her nightgown to her chest.

"You know what?" she asked. She would make him say it. She still could not believe he knew. No one could know and not say anything. He had come home on time tonight and they'd had dinner together. How could he sit through a whole dinner with her and not say anything? How could he have sat through so many dinners, gotten through so many days, and still kept quiet?

Elliot stepped toward her, his face and neck blistering from rage, and Leah saw James's face in his. She saw the recklessness, the fury, the need to lash out. She stepped back, but then Elliot turned from her and lunged for the bed. He yanked the blankets off and threw them on the floor. Then he grabbed the pillows, flung them hard against the mattress, then hurled them across the room. He stared back at her, burned her with his gaze, then, in one viciously graceful move, swiped his arm across the dresser, knocking over frames and bottles of perfume. Glass shattered on the hardwood floor and liquid seeped into the wood, bombarding the room with fragrances.

Elliot looked around wildly. He started toward her and Leah jumped back, but then he turned and ran to the closet. He flung open the door and grabbed one of Leah's blouses. He ripped it off the hanger, then hurled it at her face.

Leah watched this man, this alien man, as he ripped off blouse after blouse and flung each one at her harder than the one before. She did not back away when the clothes hit her. She took every shot, was somehow relieved at the stinging on her cheeks, as if, after all, she was getting what she'd always thought she deserved.

She stood in silence, in awe, in dreamlike fear. Elliot went through the entire closet, ripped out every piece of her clothing. When he was through, he picked up her shoes and sailed them right for her head. Leah screamed and ducked and then, for the first time, understood that he hated her and ran out of the room.

He was faster and he grabbed her before she could get to the bathroom to lock herself inside. He pulled her into the kitchen, flipped on the glaring fluorescent lights, and fixed her with a stare that chilled her.

"I know you've been seeing James Arlington for three years," he said, the words straight and precise as arrows. "I know you've gone to him every Tuesday and Thursday night and screwed his brains out in his office. I know you went to him the day we got home from the cabin."

Leah slumped, and as if every word were a fist pounding on her head, she fell toward the floor. By the time he was through, she was down on her knees, crying. He stared at her, seemed to finally see her through his fury, and then pushed her away in disgust. She had to brace herself to keep from crashing into the kitchen cabinets.

"I've always known!" Elliot shouted. "You thought I was a fool, that I'd stopped looking at you. But I was always looking. Always!"

"So why didn't you do anything?" Leah shouted back up at him.

His eyes were wide, frenzied, and Leah pulled herself up. She backed into the corner of the kitchen.

"Because I loved you," he said, his anger turning to pain. He started crying, miming sounds with his mouth. Leah was both repulsed and drawn to him. She didn't know a thing about him, she realized in that instant. She had not known he was capable of shouting, of going crazy, of ransacking their bedroom. She had not known he could feel so much pain, that he must have been feeling it all along.

"Because," he went on when he could, "I thought it would pass. I thought you'd come back to me."

"I never left you," Leah said.

Elliot's head jerked up and his tears stopped abruptly. The knives sat on the counter by his hand and he pulled out a steak knife. Leah's eyes widened as he fingered the blade.

"You think I'm crazy," he said. "You think I'd hurt you."

"I don't know what to think."

He stepped toward her, smiling, the knife still in his hand. She raised her hand to her mouth, and then Elliot quickly turned and threw the knife across the room like a carnival performer. It landed in the sofa and stuck out like an extremity.

"I saw him open the door to you," Elliot said, grabbing her arm. "His fancy silk robe was hanging open. I could see him from the road. I kept thinking, 'She won't walk in. Leah would be sickened by a display like that.' But you weren't. You were eating it up."

"He makes me feel things!" Leah shouted. She was the one who was crying now. "He wants me. He's excited by me. You can't even—"

They stared at each other and, for a moment, Elliot came back to her. His face crumbled, the anger disintegrated, and she saw him, her husband. She touched his cheek.

"Oh, El, we've got to stop this."

He jerked away at her touch and stood up straight. He turned around and walked back to the bedroom. He looked at the mess in confusion, as if he couldn't remember what he had done. Then he walked to the closet, pulled out the suitcase, and opened it up on the bed.

Leah came in and stood by the door. She thought, *I'm dreaming. If anyone's going to leave, it will be me.* But as she thought this, Elliot packed his underwear and socks and shirts and pants in his suitcase and then snapped it shut.

He walked past her without a word. He set the suitcase down by the front door and then walked into the dining room. He took his briefcase off the table and walked out the door.

And don't miss these heart-stopping
romances from Bantam Books,
on sale in September:

THIEF OF HEARTS

by the nationally bestselling author

Teresa Medeiros

"Teresa Medeiros writes rare love stories
to cherish."
—*Romantic Times*

COURTING MISS HATTIE

by the highly acclaimed

Pamela Morsi

"A refreshing new voice in romance."
—*New York Times* bestselling author Jude Deveraux

VIRGIN BRIDE

by the sensational

Tamara Leigh

"Tamara Leigh writes fresh, exciting and
wonderfully sensual historical romance."
—*New York Times* bestselling author Amanda Quick

OFFICIAL RULES

To enter the sweepstakes below carefully follow all instructions found elsewhere in this offer.

The **Winners Classic** will award prizes with the following approximate maximum values: 1 Grand Prize: $26,500 (or $25,000 cash alternate); 1 First Prize: $3,000; 5 Second Prizes: $400 each; 35 Third Prizes: $100 each; 1,000 Fourth Prizes: $7.50 each. Total maximum retail value of Winners Classic Sweepstakes is $42,500. Some presentations of this sweepstakes may contain individual entry numbers corresponding to one or more of the aforementioned prize levels. To determine the Winners, individual entry numbers will first be compared with the winning numbers preselected by computer. For winning numbers not returned, prizes will be awarded in random drawings from among all eligible entries received. Prize choices may be offered at various levels. If a winner chooses an automobile prize, all license and registration fees, taxes, destination charges and, other expenses not offered herein are the responsibility of the winner. If a winner chooses a trip, travel must be complete within one year from the time the prize is awarded. Minors must be accompanied by an adult. Travel companion(s) must also sign release of liability. Trips are subject to space and departure availability. Certain black-out dates may apply.

The following applies to the sweepstakes named above:

No purchase necessary. You can also enter the sweepstakes by sending your name and address to: P.O. Box 508, Gibbstown, N.J. 08027. Mail each entry separately. Sweepstakes begins 6/1/93. Entries must be received by 12/30/94. Not responsible for lost, late, damaged, misdirected, illegible or postage due mail. Mechanically reproduced entries are not eligible. All entries become property of the sponsor and will not be returned.

Prize Selection/Validations: Selection of winners will be conducted no later than 5:00 PM on January 28, 1995, by an independent judging organization whose decisions are final. Random drawings will be held at 1211 Avenue of the Americas, New York, N.Y. 10036. Entrants need not be present to win. Odds of winning are determined by total number of entries received. Circulation of this sweepstakes is estimated not to exceed 200 million. All prizes are guaranteed to be awarded and delivered to winners. Winners will be notified by mail and may be required to complete an affidavit of eligibility and release of liability which must be returned within 14 days of date on notification or alternate winners will be selected in a random drawing. Any prize notification letter or any prize returned to a participating sponsor, Bantam Doubleday Dell Publishing Group, Inc., its participating divisions or subsidiaries, or the independent judging organization as undeliverable will be awarded to an alternate winner. Prizes are not transferable. No substitution for prizes except as offered or as may be necessary due to unavailability, in which case a prize of equal or greater value will be awarded. Prizes will be awarded approximately 90 days after the drawing. All taxes are the sole responsibility of the winners. Entry constitutes permission (except where prohibited by law) to use winners' names, hometowns, and likenesses for publicity purposes without further or other compensation. Prizes won by minors will be awarded in the name of parent or legal guardian.

Participation: Sweepstakes open to residents of the United States and Canada, except for the province of Quebec. Sweepstakes sponsored by Bantam Doubleday Dell Publishing Group, Inc., (BDD), 1540 Broadway, New York, NY 10036. Versions of this sweepstakes with different graphics and prize choices will be offered in conjunction with various solicitations or promotions by different subsidiaries and divisions of BDD. Where applicable, winners will have their choice of any prize offered at level won. Employees of BDD, its divisions, subsidiaries, advertising agencies, independent judging organization, and their immediate family members are not eligible.

Canadian residents, in order to win, must first correctly answer a time limited arithmetical skill testing question. Void in Puerto Rico, Quebec and wherever prohibited or restricted by law. Subject to all federal, state, local and provincial laws and regulations. For a list of major prize winners (available after 1/29/95): send a self-addressed, stamped envelope entirely separate from your entry to: Sweepstakes Winners, P.O. Box 517, Gibbstown, NJ 08027. Requests must be received by 12/30/94. DO NOT SEND ANY OTHER CORRESPONDENCE TO THIS P.O. BOX.

Don't miss these fabulous Bantam women's fiction titles

Now on Sale

THE LAST BACHELOR
by Betina Krahn

"One of the genre's most creative writers. Her ingenious romances always entertain and leave readers with a warm glow." —Romantic Times

___ 56522-2 $5.99/$7.50 in Canada

WICKED PLEASURES
by Penny Vincenzi

The smash British bestseller by the author of Old Sins. "A superior three-star novel. An impressive, silky-smooth saga." —Sunday Telegraph, London

___ 56374-2 $5.99/not available in Canada

PRINCE OF WOLVES
by Susan Krinard

"Quite possibly the best first novel of the decade... Susan Krinard has set the standard for today's fantasy romance." —Affaire de Coeur

___ 56775-6 $4.99/$5.99 in Canada

WHISPERED LIES
by Christy Cohen

For years Leah Shaperson had been trapped in a marriage devoid of passion. Then a stranger's tantalizing touch awakened her desires, and she found that she'd do anything to feel wanted once more. But she would soon learn that the price of forbidden pleasure is steep...

___ 56786-1 $5.50/$6.99 in Canada

Ask for these books at your local bookstore or use this page to order.

❑ Please send me the books I have checked above. I am enclosing $ _____ (add $2.50 to cover postage and handling). Send check or money order, no cash or C. O. D.'s please.

Name _____

Address _____

City/ State/ Zip _____

Send order to: Bantam Books, Dept. FN146, 2451 S. Wolf Rd., Des Plaines, IL 60018

Allow four to six weeks for delivery.

Prices and availability subject to change without notice.

FN 146 9/94